"In this hilariously original narrative, Jory Post puts an entirely new and original twist on the concept of biography, causing us to wonder where truth lies and where it does not."

Peter Ferry
author of *Travel Writing* and *Old Heart*

"Jory Post has written an imaginative, witty, and surreal work that manages to be precise, profound, and heartbreaking, too. There is a Smith in all of us."

Syed (Smith) Afzal Haider
author of *To Be With Her* and *Life of Ganesh*

"Jory's writing is full of inventiveness and wit in this daring literary *tour de force*. Personas and personalities give insights into their gritty and tender lives in these fictional tales that as a whole make up this fictography. My favorite is BookSmith, but it's easy to find more than one Smith to love in this engaging cast of characters."

Catherine Segurson
founder and editor of the literary journal *Catamaran*

"A fairy tale of sorts about people whom you too may know or will be glad to meet on these pages. You'll be brought in to the lives of the desperate and the ingenious. Grab a coffee or the Baileys, pull up a chair, and take a listen."

Patrice Vecchione
author of *My Shouting, Shattered, Whispering Voice:*
A Guide to Writing Poetry & Speaking Your Truth

Smith: An Unauthorized Fictography

Jory Post

Published by Paper Angel Press
paperangelpress.com

ISBN 978-1-953469-40-3 (Trade Paperback)

10 9 8 7 6 5 4 3 2 1

FIRST EDITION

CONTENTS

Preface

I'M AWARE THAT THE READERS AND CRITICS and those librarians keen on keeping the Dewey decimal system clean and in order were confused, felt a little blindsided and off balance, when I called my book *Smith: An Unauthorized Fictography*, and gave my author name as Smith. Not two names so it could be easily found on a shelf or ordered from a catalogue. Not one unique name like Cher or Prince that's easy to find. But I make no apologies. It wasn't my original intent, when I set out with microphone and questions and notebooks and pens, to create a project that would actually confuse and make some, if not many, uncomfortable and wiggling in their seats not only while reading, but even more so after reading. But that's okay with me, and that's why I'm writing this opening statement — this filter one can use to think about how to think when reading these lines, to tell folks that it's not that I don't care about my readers and critics, but more so that I care about you so much that I don't want to make it easy for you, don't want to give you another spoonful of pablum or prescription of Valium that will make today and tomorrow easier for you.

You ask about the strangeness of the title. I say no stranger than any other title. What's a fictography, you ask? Read it and then you tell me. How much of this story is an autobiography? How much of it is biography? What percentage is fiction? I can't answer those questions, have no idea when I piece together a sentence and a paragraph or a thread that runs for pages, how much of it I remember hearing, and how much of it creeps in through osmosis. All I can say is that everything I write begins in the shadows — the shadows of truth, the shadows of dreams, the shadows of memories that I've lived, been told, and seen pictures of. If what I've written is simply a shadow of the truth, that's good with me.

And what about Smith, you say? What about Smith? I say back to you. You tell me. Do you get a sense of Smith? Maybe you know Smith, worked with Smith, slept with Smith. Gave Smith a dollar bill on a street corner when a sign saying "Please and Thank You" was held up. Are these characters real, you ask? All I can say is that the microphone is real. The recordings on the tapes are real. The people who agreed to be interviewed say they've provided me with truth that is real. My research conducted in the Special Collections departments of libraries across the country is real. The letters I've read from one real person to another real person are sometimes the most real words I have seen anywhere. Am I Smith? you ask. Are you Smith? I ask back.

I must stop here, for if I ramble on too long, let this preface drift into and become the first chapter, I may reveal too much too soon. And that is not for me to do. That is the task and joy or heartache of those I interviewed to share with you at their will. It is your task to take their words as you will, do with them what you wish, allow them to fester in your own shadows, or accept them as the joyful gift in the spirit in which they were given.

So enjoy. Don't worry about the word "unauthorized" in the title. That simply means that I asked no one for permission. I authorized it myself, if you will, but no other family member, no Smith, was required to give me approval for fear of being sued if they didn't like what I said.

Sincerely,
Smith

1

INTERVIEW WITH ESTHERSMITH

THE AUTHOR FIDDLED WITH THE MICROPHONE, adjusted levels on the Apple recording program.

"Can you say something before we start so I can test the sound?"

The woman showed the familiar wrinkled smile the author had become accustomed to. The author knew what to expect and waited, had learned so much about patience since spending time with this woman born during the Roaring Twenties.

"Dear, you know by now that if I say anything at all, it means we've already started, because at this colossal age I could easily fall asleep or fall over mid-sentence."

She nodded, adjusted the sound levels as the woman spoke, leaned over the microphone herself and, speaking with a stage whisper, said, "Esther Smith — Session 1, November 1, 2019."

Esther continued, "Do you mind if we start with a poem today?"

Pointing a finger at Esther and nodding, the interviewer sat back in her chair, pulled the blue Pigma Micron .30mm pen from her pocket, and placed on her lap her notebook, where she wrote the date at the top of a blank page. She preferred to remove her voice from the tape whenever possible, capture the words of the woman without her own interruptions, although occasionally she had to prompt as needed.

"I love this poet. I love most everything he's ever written."

The author scribbled a note: *What don't you love by this poet?*

She looked up and watched Esther stiffen her back, preparing herself for a recitation. Lifting the reading glasses attached to the beaded necklace to her nose, she shifted her weight in the wheelchair, made her back as stiff and straight as she could manage, brought the book to eye level, tilted her nose a little toward the ceiling, and cleared her throat.

"'Daybreak.'" Again she cleared her throat. "'On the tidal mud, just before sunset …'"

After she finished the final line, Esther slid her nose down and peered over her glasses at the author. The author knew Esther was gauging her response to the words, had done this with her numerous times over the last year.

"I'll read it again."

And she did. When she finished, she placed the eagle feather between the two pages to mark the spot and placed the book gently on the small table beside her chair.

"The image of those starfish disappearing into the sand moves me every time. I have the scene visualized. I know the beach. I've been there many times. I've watched the sunset there more times than my years. Can you imagine it? Starfish increasing their receptivity to gravity and sucking themselves down into the sand? And then you imagine that they really are gone, but you know better. Those things that disappear in our lives, that pretend to be invisible, to keep us at bay from those sorrows and pains."

She reached over and patted the book. "Galway Kinnell. He died a few years ago at eighty-seven. A very insightful man. Did you ever read him?"

The author shook her head.

"Have you ever heard of him?"

Again, no.

"Well then, do me a favor." She pointed at the wall of books to her left. "Third shelf. That's the Kinnell shelf. Grab me any book that looks interesting to you."

Rather than ask questions like "What is it you're looking for?" or "Did you know him?" she stood and remained quiet, trusted the answers would come at Esther's pace, in an order that made sense to her, not a thing the author needed to be concerned with ordering herself.

The author walked to the bookshelf, saw a title on a spine that stood out, *Mortal Acts, Mortal Words,* slipped it out of its assigned spot on the shelf — which at quick glance appeared to be arranged alphabetically — and held it out to Esther.

Esther shook her head and shooed her away. "No, no. That's yours now. You must have a Kinnell in your collection. Simply must."

The author opened the book to the title page and saw a note and signature:

To my sweet Esther —
I will remember you fondly.
— Galway

As the author considered breaking her code of silence to protest and question, Esther filled in some blanks.

"I met him at a poetry reading in Vermont in 1980, just before the book was released. He was fifty-three; I was a little older. After the reading, during the Q and A, he liked the question I asked. I could see it in his smile, his sparkling eyes, and, when I took my place at the end of the book-signing line, allowing at least a dozen others to move ahead of me so I could maintain the final position, he looked up, pen in hand, and said, 'Do you like Drambuie?' I lied and said 'Yes,' and we spent the next few days together." She wagged her bony finger at the author. "And don't argue with me. Allow me the pleasure of gifting you this treasure. I have few pathways of pleasure left and giving my treasured possessions to friends whom I know will appreciate them as I do helps me to complete my stay."

They sat for a few minutes in quiet as the digital recorder captured the silence, the author jotting down a few notes. *Where did you stay? Was he married? Did you hear from him again?* And Esther closed her eyes, eyeballs behind the skin moving rapidly, recalling what the author imagined was a vivid scene from her past.

Esther's eyes opened, moved around the room, the bookshelves, the author, the microphone, the Galway Kinnell book in the author's hands, reminding Esther where she was, who she was.

"Yes. I'm still here. It's another glorious day. I woke up once again this morning, enjoyed my two cups of caffeinated coffee at breakfast along with two cheddar cheese scones, the ones with green scallions and a dash of cayenne pepper that my friend Lenny bakes and brings by once a week." Esther looked at a cup on her table and reached over to lift it. She brought it close to her nose and sniffed. "Oh, this'll perk me up." She took a healthy swig and the author watched as her eyes lit up and she smiled. "Do you like Baileys Cream?"

The author shook her head.

"I do so love it. It's what we would sneak from our parents' cupboard when Mom went out dancing with her friends on Saturday nights. Sweet sixteen we weren't. My brother and I would pour out an inch or so into a measuring cup, maybe a quarter of a cup, split it between two shot glasses, toast each other, and toss it back. We must have been fourteen and fifteen then. It must have been '41, maybe '42. Dad was in the Navy, stationed on the USS Nevada. He was in Pearl Harbor when they got hit by one torpedo and six bombs, but they got away, not like some of those other poor sailors. I think it's what drove Mom to drink like she did, and dance like she did, with sailors on leave, maybe to remind her of Dad, maybe to forget him. Glen, my brother, would refill the empty measuring cup with milk and put a metal funnel in the Baileys Cream jar to return the volume to the same place it was before we pilfered it. Dad survived it, eventually came home, and the Baileys was replaced by harder alcohol — always a bottle of Johnnie Walker, which was a little harder to doctor, especially when you had someone home who was a connoisseur of the flavor."

The author looked at the screen and marked down the time when Esther had begun this story. Esther kept talking but watched the author looking at the screen and jotting down notes in her notebook.

"Have I told you this story before?" The author shook her head as she wrote: *Ignore this section — repetitious.*

"It's beginning to sound familiar to me, like I told someone else about it recently, about how Dad would come home shit-faced drunk after the war and find something to kick when he came through the door. Never us, not me or Glen or Mom. Usually a chair, because he was handy and could fix it the next day. Once the dog got it upside the head and stayed hidden in the laundry room after that. Maybe I dreamed it sometime this week. I have more dreams these days than I used to. I can be sitting right here in this damn wheelchair, fall asleep, and wake up with a slide of drool down my chin, thinking I'm maybe ten years old and just walked up from the creek with my friend Lisbeth with a string of crawdads and catfish that we'd hand off to Mom to clean for supper. Mom would send us upstairs to the bathtub to clean up before Dad got home, and most times Glen would be trying to look in through the keyhole and I wanted to shoot the soap dispenser in his eye, but Lisbeth was a bit of a showoff and told me no and stood straight up out of the tub with nothing but dripping skin, waving her naked body at Glen through that keyhole, even though back then we had nothing much to be waving at anybody. I liked taking those baths with Lisbeth. Not with Glen looking in though. No telling what he might say to Mom or Dad. No, sometimes I'd cover up the keyhole before we got in that steaming water and then Lisbeth and I would slip and slide all over each other's skin like we were a couple of baby sea lions playing together in the ocean."

The author watched as Esther flicked something from her eye with a knuckle.

"I lost track of her after junior high and her family moved to Ohio. I wrote one letter. She didn't write back. Oh well. But what were you and I supposed to talk about today?"

The author looked up from her notepad. At some point in their sessions, Esther would always say this, would always use the word "supposed" as if she were off-track, as if she had been rambling, even though the author had made it clear in the beginning — and every time since — that they weren't "supposed" to talk about anything, that Esther could talk about whatever she wanted to talk about. Every word she recorded about Esther was gold, was exactly what she was looking for. She hoped that would continue.

"Oh, yeah. I remember now."

Esther would always remember what she thought she was supposed to talk about, and would start at the beginning of a new event in her life: a new thought that could emerge from another word, a noise in the room, feedback from the microphone, a spot on her skin.

"What's that book you're holding?"

The author held up the Galway Kinnell book and Esther lowered her reading glasses.

"You know, I asked him about that once. I asked him whom he was making love to, and he corrected me by saying '*With*, not *to*,' and I ignored him and asked if they were his own footsteps or somebody else's? He laughed and didn't answer my question, but posed another, saying, 'Have you ever tiptoed away from someone you just made love with?' and I felt my hot face blush, amazed at how he was able to tap a corkscrew right into people's heads and watch them drain, maple syrup flowing out at first touch.

"I used to own that book … but that's not what we're supposed to talk about today. We're supposed to talk about my books, not other people's books. We want to talk about the ideas of people who are alive, not dead people like Galway Kinnell. Did I tell you I don't love everything he did? Mostly I mean everything he wrote. I do like that he once said he aspired to write poetics that 'could be understood without a graduate degree.' I very much like that he said that, but what I didn't like so much was his tendency toward self-mockery."

The author didn't care so much about Galway Kinnell's self-mockery, was hoping Esther would finally begin to talk about her own books, because if there really was something she was "supposed" to talk about — or at least that the author hoped she would talk about, without gentle persuasion — it was Esther's own books. For eleven sessions now, over thirty hours of recorded words, mostly Esther's monologue, she had at least once in every session suggested that she was supposed to talk about something else. The author wasn't sure Esther would ever talk about her own books, but this was the closest she'd come.

"In which of my books did I talk about the Baileys Cream Glen and I siphoned out of my parents' alcohol cupboard?"

She looked to the author for some hint. The author had read every one of Esther's books multiple times and knew there was never a mention of the Baileys Cream incidents, other than what she had shared on the recordings. The author wondered if there might be an unfinished manuscript in existence. A book that Esther Smith was planning to finish, and she had lost either the interest, the memories, or the manuscript itself.

The author stayed stone-faced, gave nothing away, gave Esther no clues about what she knew or didn't know about the contents of her books.

"When Glen and I were fourteen and fifteen, we used to sneak into the liquor cabinet where the Baileys Cream was kept."

2

INTERVIEW WITH JUSTSMITH

WHEN THE AUTHOR CONTACTED HIM through the internet and mentioned the project, and how much time it might take, and the stipend she could offer, he had agreed to complete the application.

Under First Name he wrote "Just," so that's what she called him; that's how she imagined him as she made her way from Santa Fe to Needles for a first interview — possibly the only interview. Whether or not a subject warranted additional interviews was always weighed carefully, usually during the recording, but she would also offer a second chance when listening to the tapes, skimming through her notes. Her grant allowed her to provide stipends to subjects, but it was not a luxurious grant, so she had to prioritize, had to be able to pay for gas and rent and buy groceries and, in some cases, book flights and rental cars to find and meet her Smiths.

When she wrote the final draft of the proposal, under the section titled "Geographical Constraints," she had said, "The geographical constraints of my project are the locales of selected subjects residing in the forty-eight contiguous states, Hawaii, and Alaska — which means my travels might take me to New York City, Iowa City, or Portland, Oregon." She hadn't, however, envisioned Needles, California, as one of her first visits.

The signs for Goose Lake let her know that Needles was a few miles down the road, and when she saw one for Jack Smith Memorial Park, she pulled in and found her way to the restrooms before looking for JustSmith. She found him where he said he'd be: under an open metal awning where a row of picnic benches sat empty except for him.

The author took a seat on the metal bench across from him, removed a pack from her back, immediately set the digital recorder and microphone on the table and, before she introduced herself, said, "I'm going to turn this on now."

He nodded. She offered him her hand, which he chose not to take.

"I prefer to avoid physical contact with strangers."

She smiled. "I understand. JustSmith, right?"

"JustSmith. Yes."

She pointed back to the concrete sign near the freeway. "Any relation to Jack Smith?"

"Not that I know of. Lived here most of my forty years and I never learned who Jack Smith was. All I know about him is he's dead."

She waited for him to continue, but it didn't happen. He pushed a toothpick around his mouth with his tongue, watched a couple of kids fishing on the lake. While she preferred to avoid her prepared questions, if he was a quiet one, she might end up listening to tapes full of her own voice, with useless information, coming away with only the knowledge that this would be a one-time interview.

"You mentioned on our call that you drive tour buses to the Laughlin casinos."

He nodded, poked the toothpick in her direction, no words.

"How'd you get into that line of work?"

"Newspaper ad."

Again, short phrases, no sentences.

"What type of people take trips to Laughlin from Needles?"

"People who like to gamble. People who like Wayne Newton."

"What kind of people like to gamble and watch Wayne Newton?"

He twisted the toothpick until it was perpendicular to and on the end of his tongue, then thrust it with a gust ten feet down the table, where it bounced and fell to the concrete.

"Dumb shits. Dumb shits who got nothing better to do with their money and haven't got a lick of sense about good music."

"And what kind of music do smart folks listen to?"

He cocked his head sideways at her and squinted. "Well, now I think you're making fun of me. First off, I don't know any smart people, so I wouldn't be able to tell you that. If you're suggesting I'm one of those smart people who listens to something different, something better, well you'd be half right. I'm not one of them smart people at all, but I do listen to something different. I definitely take my bus over there when Marshall Tucker's in town. Not Jay and the fucking Americans. And not Tony Orlando or Neil Sedaka. Give me Marshall Tucker, though, and I'll give you a ride on my bus."

Damn. Almost a whole paragraph.

"So, JustSmith. What do you do when you're not driving to Laughlin?"

"I hold interviews in the Jack Smith Memorial Park with pretty young things contemplating their navels and other people's navels."

"If you think that, why come? What made you agree to meet me here?"

"The hundred bucks you promised me."

"Really? That's it. No curiosity about the project?"

"Honey, when you live in Needles, you learn how to be a good catfish. You scavenge where the scavenging is good. A hundred bucks to talk with you a little is pretty good. I could give two shits about your project."

She wanted to say "a little" is right. Am I going to get my money's worth for this eight-hour drive and my hundred dollars? But she didn't. Wasn't this part of what she was looking for? JustSmith being JustSmith.

"Didn't you tell me you also give some tours around here, tell folks about the history?"

"I do, indeed."

"Can you tell me a little more?" She couldn't help but give a little lilt to "little."

He grinned, pulled another toothpick from his denim jacket and slipped it on his tongue. "I usually charge a hundred dollars for that."

"Well, I guess I'm in luck." He was getting to her.

"How about you show me my hundred dollars first."

She removed the hundred-dollar bill from the front pocket of her Levi's and set it on top of the recorder.

He waited a second, then bent over and reached under the table. Not knowing what the hell he was doing, if he had a gun or a knife, she quickly looked under the table and saw a cooler, saw his hand slip into it and remove two Lone Star beers.

"Thirsty?"

She was thirsty and her funders could probably give her a dozen reasons why she shouldn't accept this drink.

"I am."

He pulled a Swiss Army knife from his coat pocket, popped the two caps off and slid one of the bottles across the metal table until it was under her chin. He was playing with her now, which was fine, but it would be better if he'd talk about it — give her something to listen to later, let her know who JustSmith was, and right now she wouldn't bet a Laughlin dollar in either direction.

She took a sip and nodded her thanks to him.

"I take folks up to the canyons. Show them things they've never seen. Tell them things they've never heard."

The author took another sip of beer.

JustSmith pointed his nose toward the hills north of town. "Mostly up there. The Dead Mountains. Picture Canyon. I know where all the petroglyphs are. And I know some of the stories. Not all of them. But these tourists don't know the difference, so I give them their money's worth, embellish a little bit, if you know what I mean."

The author nodded, drank more beer, leaned in on her elbows.

"You know about the petroglyphs?" he asked.

"Just a little. Tell me."

He proffered his bottle and she clinked it. "Jedediah Strong Smith was the first white person to find them, back in 1826. He was with a group of guys trapping fur and they come across this gorgeous little spot with a spring and all of these carved rocks and he writes it down in his journal and names the place Picture Canyon. The petroglyphs survived mostly because the road was too small and twisty for wagons and other forms of transportation, so they steered away from Picture Canyon and made their main pathway on what's now called Mojave Road."

He bent over again and returned with two more Lone Stars, removed the caps and slid another one in her direction. She finished hers and slid it toward him and took the new one, the coolness from the ice chest feeling good on her hot hand.

"You take your Laughlin bus on the Picture Canyon tours?"

He cackled. "Oh, god, no. Couldn't make it around the first bend in that whale. No. I've got me a Dodge van I modified. I took out all the windows, torched out most of the metal, except a few shafts on each side, enough to hold the roof on, and I have my own little Safari wagon. Except we won't find any lions or elephants out here."

"What will we find?"

"Some of the prettiest country you've ever seen. Coyotes. Mountain lions. Rattlesnakes. Lots of rattlesnakes. One of the petroglyphs out there is a rattlesnake. Legend has it it's Humasereha — a gigantic rattler and medicine man whose rattling tail made rain and thunder. Just stories, though."

She smiled. "Just stories by JustSmith."

He smiled back. "So much easier that way. Anybody who needs to know my name either wants something from me or wants to put me in jail, so JustSmith is just fine."

She looked out at the Dead Mountains, and imagined him with a van full of tourists from New Jersey listening to his stories about the Mojave Indians, though he probably gave them a hundred dollars' worth of words and more. She felt like she was close herself. Maybe JustSmith just might warrant a second interview, and maybe even a third.

The author had to think hard when he offered her the third beer. What was she doing here? What were the boundaries of her research? She had written down the required objectives, goals, and outcomes and how they'd be measured, but she really had no idea what she'd discover, whom she'd discover. All she knew is she had two years to do it, whatever it was, and JustSmith had turned out to be worth the drive across the desert.

3

INTERVIEW WITH ADAMSMITH

"D O YOU WANT ME TO PRETEND, maybe AdamSmith?" The author fiddled with the recording equipment. She offered a fake smile.

"No. Just be yourself. We'll figure it out. Talk about anything and everything."

"No prompts? No lists of questions? Just go for it?"

"If you want, I can prompt you."

"I want."

The author opened her notebook reluctantly. "Tell me about the single most important event in your life."

"Seriously? Just one?"

At first, the author did not respond, tried to wait him out. He waited as well.

"Start with one," she conceded.

"Let's see. You might think it was the day my wife walked out on me to be with her dentist boss, or maybe the next day when I decided to unload my gun and not drive down to the dental complex and blow his and her brains out, mostly because of the kids who might be in the office. I didn't want them traumatized for life because of the infidelity and recklessness of the adults around them. Both of those incidents were defining moments for me. Changed my life forever. Made me the sweet, nonjudgmental man you see here today. But nowhere near the single most important event in my life. Is this the kind of thing you're looking for? Is your recorder picking up this brilliance?"

The author nodded affirmatively to both questions.

"Help yourself to refreshments." She had read that having finger food available during interviews might make subjects more at ease, keep their mouths moving. She had brought red plastic bowls, and filled them from bags of peanut M&Ms and that Asian mix with wasabi peanuts and sesame sticks, accompanied by a bottle of Perrier.

"Not for me, thanks. I try to eat a little healthier than this. Maybe some water."

He twisted the cap off the bottle and filled half of one of the plastic cups she'd brought.

"Where were we? The most important moment in my life. Makes me walk back through every phase."

That's good. That's what she was looking for. She poured herself a half glass of the Perrier — another tip: establish a sense of camaraderie.

"I was in Vietnam and I didn't get killed. There were lots of those moments. They could qualify. That I came home physically unscarred. Or that I didn't come home emotionally unscarred. That I'm a poster child for PTSD. Those were all big moments. Still are. Big moments that reverberate almost daily. But I don't let that stuff make me who I am. Like so many of my brothers who wallow in it. Get over it, I tell them. Live this goddamn life.

So, maybe it's when I took advantage of the GI Bill and went back to school. Maybe it's when I graduated college, first in my family to do so. Or maybe the first day I stepped into a classroom in front of a bunch of snot-nosed kids. By the way, I don't have a gun. Haven't touched one since 'Nam. Don't own one. So you'll have to figure out what's fiction and fact once you sit down to listen to this shit that's pouring out of me. I mean, you mostly know the true parts, or you wouldn't have picked me for your study. My wife did leave me. Not for anyone special that I know of. More because she couldn't stand waking up to the screaming and sweating body next to her every night. She didn't know what to do with it. Of course, neither did I, but I had no choice. Not about to kill myself, given the miracle that I'm still breathing, and all. But she had to leave.

"I could go on with the many amazing moments in my life that aren't 'the one' — the one and only special moment, like the day I was selected as a recipient of the Christa McAuliffe Award. Another life changer. Took me out of the classroom and paid my salary to be creative, to develop projects to enhance the educational lives of students and teachers, to build robots and virtual field trips and talk with amazing folks at NASA and NOAA. Never went back to the classroom, kept finding new ventures and funding sources that helped me lose those nightmares, create some new dreams for me and others. But you know all this. That's why you're here. Why you brought candy and bubbly water. So, what is this study about?"

The author took a sip of Perrier, had known this moment would come, had known from her research that the interviewee might flip the discussion, begin asking the questions instead of answering them. For Smith #3, she had her prepared answer. It would change for each of them, depending on their life circumstances, but for him it was: "Simply studying the thoughts and actions of teachers who went on to pursue other interests." Another sip from the Perrier. She wanted to grab a handful of

M&Ms, but, in trying to tighten the bond between them to loosen him up, she wanted to avoid eating the food he had labeled as unhealthy.

"Yeah, I know, that's what you told me on the phone. That thing I'm supposed to believe. But I don't believe it. I think there's more to it than that. Maybe I'll find out in five years if you ever publish this thing."

"My funding's only for one year."

"Yeah, but it'll take you three years to figure out what you've got, then write it up. And when you publish it, maybe that will be the single most important event in your life."

She smiled. He was clever, had gotten back to the topic at hand, had never really moved too far away from it, just moved into and around a few rabbit holes before popping his head back out, remembering exactly where he was and who was there with him.

"And it wasn't when I married my second wife, who is the absolute love of my life, or the births of our two children, whom I adore. And it wasn't the supreme sadness and depression that overwhelmed me for six months when my mother died. And it wasn't when the Giants won the World Series for the second time in three years — though that was big, very big, and for the greater glory of the team and San Francisco and the West Coast, I might consider giving up my own personal most important moment and trade it in for the Giants' amazing feat. But no, I'm not that generous person who relinquishes all claims by the ego to make way for the global consciousness required for enlightenment.

"I love my Giants, but I will always remain true to myself, not settle for some second-rate moment, though highly important, like my biking trip through Europe with my GoPro hooked to my forehead, broadcast live through my website titled — wait, let me modify the name of the site for the sake of the interview, before you have to do it yourself — broadcast live through my website titled 'Smith Rides Europe.' I had over two million followers trekking with me. I posted lessons for students and teachers throughout the two-month trip, lessons on European geography, the technical specifications of bike maintenance, how and where to clean clothes while on the road, the mathematics of altitude and speed and number of calories required to maintain body weight when biking eight hours a day. While important, to me, and I hope to the students and teachers who followed me and learned something, it was not the number-one defining moment in my life. But I could go on with the amazingly wonderful and awful things I've experienced so far, and keep you guessing, or I could just get to it right now."

The author smiled and couldn't resist grabbing three M&Ms and tossing them into her mouth. Smith #3 followed quickly, grabbing a large handful and throwing it into his mouth.

"Jeez, I was wondering how long you'd be able to hold out thinking you needed to mimic my interests to get me to talk. I love my M&Ms. I will need to provide you with a little more context before finally answering your question.

"My mother was a young farm girl just outside Lawrence, Kansas, in 1950, milking cows and shearing sheep and helping out with family chores while they helped her out with tuition at KU, that would be the University of Kansas for the uninitiated. My dad had come to KU on a track scholarship, ran the one-hundred- and two-hundred-yard sprints until he fell in an event against University of Iowa and strained his Achilles tendon. They met in an American literature class during their second semester, Dad in a cast, Mom helping him out with his books, given his hands being occupied on crutches.

"One thing led to another, and they weren't big on condoms back then, but were big on passion, so that night at the drive-in, while watching *Father of the Bride*, with the magic of Spencer Tracy and Joan Bennett and Elizabeth Taylor, well they ended up in the backseat of Dad's roommate's 1948 Dodge D-24 Deluxe two-door sedan, meaning they had to climb over the seats and fall onto the back cushions, and, as Dad tells it, all clothes were off in less than twenty seconds except his socks, and just about the time Stanley T. Banks, played by Spencer Tracy, says, 'Who giveth this woman? . . . but she's not a woman. She's still a child. And she's leaving us,' according to Dad, that is when that one specific sperm of my father's burst out in all its passion and glory and found its way to and embedded itself in that one specific egg from that one specific ovary that split and grew and became me over the next nine months. That moment is the most important in my life, because without it, the miracle of me would never have occurred. I would never have experienced all the other moments I've mentioned, and not mentioned yet, if it hadn't been for the passion enjoyed by my parents in the backseat of Ricky Mueller's Dodge.

"By the way, I know you give your subjects names or numbers in these kinds of studies. What are you calling me in this study?"

The interviewer shifted in her chair, not sure she should give anything away about her study, the real intent, anything at all. But she did. "You're my third. So, I'll call you Smith Number Three if you don't come up with something." More M&Ms and another sip of Perrier.

"Really. That's fascinating. Fascinating that I'm the third, and fascinating to use one of the most common names in America. Well, I'm happy to play that role for you. I'll go with AdamSmith."

4

Interview with JoeSmith

"**G**OOD THING YOU FOUND ME HERE TODAY. I leave tomorrow for a couple days in San Francisco, then home for a few weeks for my new assignment."

"Can you say where we are now, and where home is, for the recorder." She tapped the recorder with the eraser end of her pencil.

"Sure. And I guess this is a good time to tell you my name: I'm Joe. You can call me JoeSmith."

The interviewer scribbled *JoeSmith* at the top of a new page in her notebook.

"We are sitting in an outside rest or dining area on the second floor of Dominican Hospital in Santa Cruz, California. You brought us lunch from the outside, because I told you during our phone call that the food here is atrocious, and it looks like you brought us food from Gayle's Rosticceria, if the name on the bag is any clue. I was born and raised in Saipan, the capital of the Northern Mariana Islands."

The interviewer thought about JoeSmith's words, and they felt stilted, like she had just told him what to say and he had said them verbatim, as if they were written down on a sheet of paper, like singing a hymn in church. She needed to relax, needed to let this all flow naturally and easily. She opened the bag and pulled out two ficelle sandwiches, a pint of potato salad, and two chocolate eclairs.

"Wow! Nice looking food."

"Dig in."

She left the recorder on, even though there wasn't much talk while they chewed. Storage space was cheap. Missing some verbal gems might be expensive.

"This is good. Just what I needed. This job is crazy sometimes. I might not get a meal until dinner or later."

With a bit of a mouthful, the interviewer said, "Tell me more about the work."

Joe was chomping down a big bite but finished it and said, "Being a traveling nurse is kind of cool. For one thing, I can pretty much go wherever I want now. I've been doing it for ten years, and I get good evaluations, so they like me and want me. And the pay is very good. Free housing, free courses. A 401k plan. Comprehensive medical insurance.

"I've been here at Dominican for about six months. I like Santa Cruz a lot, because I love to surf. Back in Saipan, there's a huge coral reef where the surf isn't any good at all, and, because it's a bit dangerous, most of us wind surf instead. But, I've taken my chances and been cut up a bit. See."

He showed the interviewer gashes on his arms and his rib cage.

"But here, I just love Steamer Lane and Pleasure Point. I'll take night shifts whenever I can so I can spend days on the water. But when you're a traveler, you pretty much take what shifts they give you. This place is pretty good. There's lots of other travelers here so we share a house down by the Crow's Nest that the company provides us. It gets a little wild and crazy at times. Nurses like to blow off a little steam. I won't mention any names though, 'cause 'Joe from Saipan' probably wouldn't be too hard to figure out and calling me a 'Smith' isn't much of a cover.

"But there are a couple of the women on the dayshift who've been taking a pole dancing class, and they installed a brass pole right in the middle of the living room, and we get the benefit of watching them practice. And they like tequila, and a couple of recreational drugs that it probably wouldn't be prudent for me to mention. And they surf, better than me, and have taught me so much.

"There are eight of us who live in this four-bedroom house and, because we have different shifts, we share beds, usually having it mapped out so we have beds to ourselves, but occasionally I might end up in bed with one of the pole dancers or Alex, if shifts don't match well. It's mostly okay, other than a little snoring and farting and sheet hogging. And there are a few fringe benefits if enough tequila's been poured."

Joe Smith stopped to gobble down the rest of the sandwich and take a few bites of potato salad.

The interviewer took time to clean up her notes and asked, "My research suggests that the traveling nurse companies like to hire folks with specialties? What's yours?"

Joe Smith crumpled up the sandwich wrapper and tossed it across the patio to a waste basket like a free throw. "Swish! The other thing I love about working in the Bay Area is that the Golden State Warriors are only an hour and a half away. I've been to most of the home games this year, and I love to watch Steph Curry, such a classy guy. But those fans drink so much beer, it's crazy. Yelling at the opposing players, yelling at guys like LeBron James. It's just crazy. Me, I stick to my ice teas with Sweet'N Low. I learned my lesson back on the island. Did you know that Budweiser has statistics that show the residents of Saipan drink more Budweiser per capita than any other place in the world? Nothing else to do there. It's a tiny place, far away from real civilization, so the folks there eat a lot, drink a lot, and screw a lot. Lots of pregnancies and babies and alcoholism. I'm glad to be gone. But I'll be glad to get back there for a visit. I miss my nieces and nephews, my parents."

He took a swallow from his drink, emptied the can, and crumpled it up before swishing it into the garbage can.

"My specialty? I'd like to say I'm a three-point specialist for the Warriors, but I'm a little too short for the real game. I play a little pickup game on my days off down at the gym at New Brighton Middle School. Mostly nurses, but a few of the high school jocks show up from Soquel High. Those guys are good. And tall. But I can keep up with them. I'm pretty strong."

He smiled and flexed his right bicep, where a tattoo reminiscent of the Pacific Islands danced as he did so.

"But, no, sadly that's not my specialty. I'm mostly an ER nurse. I practice Buddhism, so I stay pretty calm within the stressful walls of the ER room, help relax the patients and some of my fellow staff with my approach to life and work. You need to keep your cool in the ER room. You see lots of crazy stuff happen to lots of crazy people: blood, bones, screamers, young kids, and folks about ready to call it quits. Because I have a holistic understanding of life and death, I stay focused and can deal with codes and have a second sense about whether someone is really at the end, by choice, or whether there is a sense of urgency to bring folks back to complete the journey. I don't talk like this when I'm on the job, but I think this way, act this way, and it helps me make the right decisions as needed. Because I'm fast and efficient with most of my bedside tasks, they often take me upstairs and use me to admit patients from the ER. They've got a nickname for me, 'Poker,' for a few reasons, but mainly because I can hit a vein the first time every time when it looks like a patient has no veins. Quick, slick, and no pain. And even though I'm in and out with new patients quicker than most, I make them feel important, make them comfortable, because I believe they are important, they're here in this traumatic entrance to a place and a bed that is unfamiliar, and they don't have their pillows they're used to, and it's my job to make them feel at home.

"So, I'm going home next week. Get to eat some of my favorite food on the planet. Have you ever seen pictures of the coconut crabs in Saipan? Sometimes you can find them just scampering across highways. Locals will pull over, jump out and throw them in their backseats or trunks. They are considered a delicacy, huge claws with lots of meat, and many of the locals consider them aphrodisiacs. Some of those suckers grow to almost three feet across. The reason we call them coconut crabs is their claws are so strong they can crack open a coconut, and they like to climb coconut trees and knock them to the ground to feed on."

He stopped for another bite of potato salad.

The interviewer asked, "Where's your next assignment, after you get your fill of coconut crabs?"

"I've been with this company, American Mobile, for almost eight years now, worked in seventy-five hospitals since I started traveling, and I've never been to the Northwest yet, so I'm looking at three to four months in Portland, right in the middle of basketball season. I've never seen the Trailblazers play yet, and I love to watch Damian Lillard shoot three-pointers. When the season's over they'll send me up to Seattle, and I plan to spend a lot of time riding ferries around the Sound up there. I like to bike ride, and the islands are supposed to be good for that, especially Lopez Island. No basketball in Seattle anymore. Had the Supersonics until 2008, but they moved to Oklahoma City. Can you imagine that? A whole team moving from the water on the Pacific Northwest to Oklahoma City? Talk about mobility." JoeSmith shook his head. "It's a crazy life we nurses and athletes have chosen."

The interviewer straightened herself in her chair. "I've just about used up all your lunch break. Anything else you'd like to share? Other things you do for fun when you're not setting IVs and saving lives?"

"You've heard most of them. Basketball. Surf. More basketball. My Buddhism. Bike riding. Oh. I have a nice camera. I take *lots* of pictures, everywhere I go, take a photojournalism approach to every new city and hospital I visit. I must have over one hundred thousand photos on a little three-terabyte disk drive I take with me wherever I go. I plan on writing a book about the life of the traveling nurse someday: a coffee-table book full of photos, cover picture of a big coconut crab wrapped around a coconut on a highway. You want to see my pictures before you leave town? Come by for a tequila? Watch some exotic pole dancing?"

The interviewer turned off the digital recorder.

5

Interview with SmithSmith

"Linda says you want to talk to me."

"Yes. Sort of. I'd actually like you to talk to me."

"Why me?"

"To be honest, I was meeting someone else here to interview during lunch and she didn't show. I had my recorder set up, and Linda saw that I was stood up, and told me you were an interesting person, and I might like to hear what you have to say. The place is closing now, and she said we could sit here while they clean up. And I'll buy you lunch."

"Linda gives me free lunch. Silver Spur is the best food in my territory."

"Can you tell me more about your territory?"

"I can. But I have some questions first? Are you going to record me?"

"Yes."

"Can you change it so my voice doesn't sound like my voice?"

"If you prefer."

"I prefer. Will my name remain anonymous?"

"It will. In fact, I name all the subjects I talk with Smith — or, I should say, they give themselves a Smith name."

"Okay. Then, my name is Smith. What do you mean by subject?"

"I call all the people I speak with 'subjects,' for the sake of the study."

"What study?"

"I really can't say more about that, but I'm very interested in having you tell me about you."

"What about my name?"

"Is Smith your first or last name?"

"It's my only name. So I guess it's both."

"Okay. Shall I call you 'SmithSmith'?"

"Sure. And you're going to give me one hundred dollars if I talk to you?"

"I am."

"You are what?"

"Going to give you one hundred dollars when we finish talking."

"That's good, because I have things I need to buy, today. Linda pays me cash every day to clean up, but today I need a little more to buy the things I need to buy."

"Great. What things do you need to buy?"

"I can't tell you that. It's top secret."

"Okay. You were going to tell me about your territory."

"That's not exactly right. You asked me to tell you about my territory. I didn't say I'd tell you."

"Will you tell me about the territory?"

"Why should I do that?"

"Because I want to know who you are. And so I can give you the hundred dollars when we're through."

"I can use one hundred dollars. I have things to buy. All I have to do is tell you about my territory and I can have my one hundred dollars?"

"Not exactly. I'd like to know all about you, have you tell me all about you. Can you do that?"

"Is that recorder on?"

"Yes."

"Are you going to ask me questions?"

"I prefer to have you just talk about yourself. I may take a few notes in my notebook here, but mostly I'll listen to what you say because I'm interested in learning more about you. If you get stuck, I may ask you questions."

"Okay. But wait. Do you work for the government? I used to work for the government and I don't trust anyone who works for the government anymore. Do you work for them?"

"Absolutely not. I work for myself. This is my study that I designed all by myself. Nobody's help."

"Okay. What do you want to know?"

"How about starting with your territory?"

"Who told you about my territory? Did Linda tell you about that? She's not supposed to say anything about that. I don't want them to know where I am."

"You mentioned earlier that Linda had the best food in your territory."

"Definitely the best food. Have you ever tried the Grazer? I get it healthy. Egg whites. No yolks for me. Clogs up these veins. Check out these biceps. I stay fit. No yolks for me. I also add avocados. Half an avocado. Has the good oils in it. It's important to substitute fruit for the home-fried potatoes. The potatoes are to die for, but they will literally kill you. You should probably skip the muffin of the day, especially on Wednesdays, which is the cinnamon bun. Get the whole wheat English muffin. No butter. And skip the coffee. Best coffee in the territory. But skip it, caffeine will kill you. Just a big glass of room-temperature water.

"I've been eating here at the Silver Spur since before Linda bought it. It's just about right in the middle of my territory. If you walk out Linda's front door, you head east down Soquel Drive. All my territory is situated along Soquel Drive, and a few side streets off Soquel Drive. Head east across the Rodeo Gulch bridge and past Oil Can Henry's which has only been there a couple of years. Great place to have your oil changed, if you have a car. I don't have a car. My territory is walkable. Don't need a car. There's no Henry working at Oil Can Henry's. It's a franchise. Walk up past the doctors' offices and the lumberyard with the forty-foot beams and the empty lot except when it's time to sell pumpkins and Christmas trees. Then you walk by the do-it-yourself car wash, which is a good place to wash your car if you have one. I don't have one. I walk everywhere.

"When you reach King's Paint store on the corner, that's the southeast corner of my territory. I don't go beyond that corner. I will cross the street, when the light's green, to get to the northeast corner of my territory, but I won't cross Forty-First Avenue. Stop right there at Kings Paint, and you always have to read what they put on their marquee sign out front, because it's usually funny. Usually making fun of some political situation or just some pun that's funny. I'll go in and talk to the folks there. I'm not good with names. Can't remember their names. Except Linda. I remember Linda's name because she's good to me. Talks to me every day. Except Sundays, because they're closed on Sundays, and I have to find someplace else in my territory to eat. And there are a few but I'll tell you about those once we cross the street and head west on the other side. Linda closes at Christmas, too, for two whole weeks, so I really have to find other places to eat then.

"When the light turns green, we're going to cross the street, but still look both ways even though they're supposed to stop because you never know when somebody's been drinking and has their senses impaired. That's another thing. Don't drink alcohol. It will kill your brain cells faster than your brain cells should die, because you're going to need them for an awful long time. I lost some of mine in Vietnam. Got a metal plate that fits inside my head. See the scar here right under my hairline?

"There's a big new shopping center they built here on the northeast corner of my territory last year. A big UPS store, in case you want to send packages to your family at Christmas or on their birthdays. I don't have any family anymore, so I don't have to send packages. But I could. I could send packages because I have lots of treasures in one of my places. Who's going to hear this recording here? I just told you about my treasures and I don't want the government to know about them. You promise that you won't let them listen to this recording? Where I told you about my treasures?"

"I promise. Nobody will hear it but me."

"Okay, then. I trust you, because you made a promise. That's another thing. It's very important to keep your promises. I promise Linda to come in every day after three o'clock and clean up the Silver Spur, make it spotless, like I used to shine my boots in the army, like I used to keep the mess hall, because I was a chef in the army. Well, they didn't call us chefs, called us cooks, but I was more like a chef because I was clever and inventive with the food and everyone loved my food. Linda keeps her promises, too. Pays me cash every day so I don't have to worry about the government getting into my affairs too much. And she promised to feed me every day, and she keeps that promise, too. Except Sundays and two weeks at Christmas.

"We pass the UPS store on the northeast corner of my territory, because I don't have any packages to send and I have enough stamps for now, and if I give treasures to people, I will just do it in person. I have them wrapped up nicely and I will just hand them to them. Like Linda. I give her presents all the time. Except at Christmas when she's gone to Hawaii for two weeks. Linda told me I could trust you, that you're the kind of person who keeps promises, so I can tell you about my treasures and my places. Once you get past the new UPS store, you pass the VW repair shop. This is a good place to look down at the ground as you walk, because people drop things when they walk down this part of my territory. They lose things from their pockets and their purses and jackets. And they're gone, so I pick them up, and they become my treasures. Unless Linda tells me she knows of someone who's lost something, then I give her treasures to return to the folks, because I don't want to own treasures that someone is missing, if I know how to get them back to them. If you have a VW this is a good place to come to get it repaired, because the guys here, I can't remember their names, are very friendly. Give me coffee on the morning walk through my territory.

"Next on our walk is the very large Honda car dealership that didn't used to be here. They say it used to be across the freeway, where I never go because I don't go past Forty-First Avenue. This is a good place to buy a new car if you like Hondas.

"Okay. We're almost to one of my places now. This is Store More America, 3711 Soquel Drive. It's okay for me to tell you that, because you promised me you wouldn't let anybody hear the tape, and it's okay anyway, because you don't know what number my unit is, and I don't tell anybody my unit number, not even Linda. I keep the key with my dog tags around my neck on this silver chain. See? Nobody touches my chain, because they don't know about it, because it's always hidden under my shirt. Just Linda knows. And now you. My unit is ten feet by ten feet; that's one hundred square feet I have to store my treasures and other things. I won't tell you where it is, because I need to keep some things secret. Like what's in my space here at the storage unit. I call it space number one because I have a second space, which we'll get to shortly. We'll walk by my storage unit and pass the Winchester Auto Parts store, which is not a good place to get car parts for your car if you have one. I don't have one. But if you do, don't buy them here because the guys who run this store are not friendly. Tell me to get out and stay out and stop loitering, even though I tell them I'm not loitering. I know what loitering means, to linger aimlessly in a place, because I have dictionaries in both my spaces, and I don't linger, and it's not aimless.

"I go into the Winchester Auto Parts store to look for treasures. I have money in my pocket. I can buy their treasures if I want, but they say I'm loitering and they're wrong. So I don't go in there anymore. I just walk on by until I get to Sweet's in the Nude which is on the corner of Rodeo Gulch Road, and I walk inside every day, because they are friendly in there, they come into Linda's and have breakfast and they are friends of Linda and I love the way the wood smells in there and they have very large treasures, ones that won't fit inside my two spaces, but I like to look at them. Sometimes maybe I think I should get a bigger storage unit so I could buy some of these bigger treasures, but my space is ten foot by ten foot and costs me one hundred seventy-eight dollars every month for rent, which is good because I get my disability check from the government every two weeks and there's plenty to pay for my space and get treasures at the Flea Market, but we're not there yet, because it's on the other side of the street.

"Now we keep heading west on Soquel Drive and we cross that Rodeo Gulch bridge again but this time we're on the other side of the street. Once we cross the bridge if you look across the street you can see Linda's Silver Spur restaurant and on the morning walk, the parking lot is full and people are sitting around outside on benches reading newspapers and drinking coffee waiting for a table because they're all full of people eating Grazers and specials of the day like huevos rancheros or sand dabs and eggs. They only have the sand dabs on special occasions, when the sand dabs are in season and Linda buys them from the fishermen. On those days, I'll pass up my healthy Grazer with egg whites and no yolks and avocado and whole wheat muffins with no butter, and instead will order the sand dabs that have been lightly fried in beer batter, and they taste so good I don't care so much about the grease they've been fried in. Because it's only about once a month she buys the sand dabs from the fishermen. On the afternoon walk the parking lot's empty because they're closed and I'm in there cleaning up and making it spic-and-span.

"We keep walking east and pass the Jelli Beanz store and the dance studio and El Chino restaurant, which is one place I eat at when I don't eat at Linda's, like for dinner because Linda isn't open for dinner. Leonardo knows what I like and when he sees me come in the front door off Soquel Drive, he nods at me and I sit at my table by the window, that seats four people, but it's only ever me at my table, unless Leonardo is not busy and comes and sits down and talks to me about treasures and things. I told Leonardo about my things, too. He promised he wouldn't say anything to anybody. That's three of you who know now. Linda, Leonardo, and you. What's your name? Does it start with an 'L' also? It's okay if it doesn't. I still trust you. Leonardo brings me a bowl of chips with a bowl of salsa that has a plastic spoon in it. I've told him that he should put a real metal spoon in the salsa bowl, and he says it's too big and would slip out, but I tell him anyway that plastic is not treasurable, that metal can be, but not plastic. Never plastic. Then he brings me my grilled chicken salad that has avocado and carrots and tomatoes and lettuce, and he always brings me two containers of blue cheese dressing because he knows what I like after all these years of me coming here to eat when I don't eat at Linda's, because she's closed for dinner. With a big glass of water, because that's what I drink. No ice. Room temperature because it's better for your body not to drink liquids that are too cold or too hot.

"If we leave El Chino's and continue or walk east, right next door is Upper Crust Pizza, and sometimes I'll grab a slice if I'm hungry, but not too much, because pizza irritates my bowels, and I don't like to have irritable bowels. But space number two is right across the street so sometimes if I wake up from my afternoon nap hungry, after I've made the rounds in walk number two, I'll go grab a vegetarian slice because I don't eat meat because meat is not good for your digestion and doesn't help when you have irritable bowels.

"When we cross the street, there's Mel's Market, where I get milk and other things I need, because my space number two is right behind Mel's, in the lot behind the chain-link fence where they store the old campers and other vehicles. They all look pretty run-down, which is why I like it for space number two, because nobody knows I'm there. In the back corner hidden between two big old rusty Winnebagos is my little Ford pickup with camper on the back, which is where I live and sleep and read my books. But that's my private place, so let's keep walking east down Soquel Drive where we pass another storage place, but I don't use them because their prices are higher and the managers aren't friendly like my place.

"We walk past the appliance store which I never go in, but behind it is the water store, which is where I buy my five-gallon jugs of water which I go through every couple of days because I drink a lot of water. See. I keep this bottle on my belt buckle because it's important to drink lots of water every day, and especially if you are making two trips a day around my territory, top to bottom, getting all that exercise and sweating, you need to replenish your body's supply. It's good to have a water store so close to space number two. You might think I should call space number two space number one because it's where I sleep and read and sometimes cook on my little hot plate, but space number one is called space number one because it's where I keep my treasures and that's what's most important to me. Look inside my jacket here. See how I've sewn in all these little pockets on the inside of the whole jacket, both sides. In each pocket I have one of my treasures, so I can hand them out to folks I meet along my walks who I like, who I think deserve one of my treasures. That's why space number two is not called space number one.

"When we continue east on Soquel Drive we pass a large open space which is usually empty and open behind a chain-link fence, except when they have the rummage sales and sell Christmas trees and pumpkins. And right on the corner is where the bus stops to give people rides to where they want to go. I never get on that bus, because I know where I want to go, and I can go there by foot, on these two strong legs, and haven't been in a motor vehicle since I was in Vietnam and don't care to ever be in one again. We'll walk by the bus stop because we don't need it, never use it, and when the light turns green, we'll cross Thurber Lane, and on the corner is Wells Fargo Bank, which is where I keep my money. It's where the government sends my checks every two weeks, and that's the only thing I ever have to do with the government, because I don't trust them, even though they send me the disability check, and help me build savings and have enough money to collect my treasures.

"Just past the bank are two more places where I get food when I need it. Garden Liquors. Don't let the name fool you. Yes, they have plenty of liquor in there, which I never drink, not since I left Vietnam, because it doesn't mix well with this metal plate up here, but they have good food here in the deli. Fresh sandwiches and soups. They have deviled eggs, but I don't eat them because of the yolks. Behind the liquor store is Angel Sweet donut shop, and I never go in there, because Angel who owns it is not very friendly to me, and if they have custard-filled maple donuts I will buy them all and devour them along with a bottle full of room-temp water because I'm kind of addicted to them and I know they are not good for my veins, so I try to avoid it, stop at the liquor store instead and get a three-bean salad if I need a snack on my afternoon walk after I've cleaned Linda's restaurant.

"Next we pass the Rabobank on the corner of Mission Drive and Soquel Drive, but I don't like the name Rabo, so I don't keep my money there. Wells Fargo is better. I like the image of the stagecoaches because I know they've been around a long time and I trust that they will take care of my money, even if it comes from the government, trust that they will promise to take care of my money for me. I won't have to get money out of the bank today because you're giving me a hundred dollars.

"We walk by more doctors' offices, lots of them, and the entrances to Dominican Hospital. I walk right by those entrances, both of them, and don't look in, and when ambulances are turning in I cover my ears and close my eyes and wait for them to pass and head back to Emergency and turn off their sirens, then I keep walking until I reach the corner, which is the northwest boundary of my territory.

"The freeway is across the street to the west, and I don't like the freeway, so I wait until the light turns green and cross the street until I reach the southwest corner of my territory, now having touched all four corners, and walk back east down Soquel Drive so I can complete my trip. There's a Union gas station on the corner, which is a good place to get gas if you have a car, which I don't, and it's the only place to get gas in my territory. I only go into their store to get a bottle of water if it's hot and my bottle is empty. By the time I pass the gas station and take a big swig of water, I'm working up some steam, not paying attention to this part of my territory too much, because I'm a little tired by now and ready to finish. So I walk quickly past the used furniture store, and the travel agency, because I don't travel anymore since coming back across the Pacific all bandaged up and mangled. No need. No interest. So why would I stop at a travel agency? I wouldn't. And I don't. And I never will. So let's just not talk about it anymore.

"Let's keep walking, quickly past the Adobe Animal Hospital and Erik's Deli. But to be fair, I will sometimes stop in at Erik's Deli to get a bowl of chili, which is not very smart of me, given my irritable bowels, but I love chili, have always loved chili since I was a kid and my mom made the best chili around, so sometimes I'll stop at Erik's when I'm thinking about my mom or dad who aren't here anymore, eat a big bowl of chili and think about both of them with each bite. But I pay for it later. I sure do. But I'm still gonna stop at Erik's and get that big bowl of chili when I feel like it, when I want to think about my parents.

"Now we cross the street at Commercial Way and walk past the chain-link fence where the United Rental store is, where you can rent a truck, if you know how to drive and have a driver's license, which I don't, well I do know how to drive, or used to know how to drive Jeeps in Vietnam, but no more, don't have a license, don't care to drive. They all drive too fast through my territory. Makes me mad. They should slow down. They should walk. It's good for them. More doctors' offices and the Sutter facility where they do what's called outpatient surgery on folks who have minor problems like having babies or knee operations where you can either leave the same day or maybe spend one night.

"Oh. Now that we're at Sutter, I'm going to tell you a very big secret that you can't tell anyone else. They have a cafeteria here that serves food to the patients who have to stay overnight. It is very good food. They have a salad bar, and they have daily specials, and they have a very good breakfast, which is where I come on some Sundays when Linda's Silver Spur is closed, and order the special breakfast sandwich of the day, which sometimes has ham or sausage on it which I take off because of the bowel thing but it's left with eggs, I order egg whites, and cheese and onions and sometimes tomatoes, and it's very good. But it's funny to think of a hospital as a restaurant, so I don't tell too many people about it, because it's kind of my secret. Just past Sutter is one of my favorite places in the territory, probably number four, space number one being the first, because of the treasures, Linda's Silver Spur being the second, because of everything there, space number two, because it's where I read and sleep, and this place, the Flea Market, which is where I spend a good portion of my day on Fridays, Saturdays, and Sundays, because those are the only days they're open. If you get here at six o'clock in the morning while it's still dark, all the cars and trucks are lined up along Soquel Drive before they open and let people in. Fridays are the best. That's when I find my best treasures. Saturdays and Sundays have more food places, not as many folks who bring their treasures. So the Flea Market is number four on my list of favorite places in the territory. Maybe number three. Maybe better than space number two, because I could probably live without sleeping and reading, but not without my treasure hunting.

"So we walk past the Flea Market, past the apartments called Villa San Carlos, where a lot of people who can't afford better places live. But I can't afford to live there. And I wouldn't want to. I don't need all those rooms. I don't need bedrooms and kitchens. Just a mattress and a light and a hot plate. Because I don't spend much time there.

"Okay. We're coming to the end of the trip. We pass the gate for Villa San Carlos and there's the antique store on the right. I go in there every day, because there are lots of folks in there with nice treasure. They're usually too expensive for my taste, but I look every day, look at every item in all of the little stores inside, spend maybe two hours between one o'clock and three o'clock, just before I walk through their parking lot and into Linda's parking lot, use the bathroom on the back porch to clean up before I go to work cleaning up the Silver Spur.

"And that's my territory. Where I collect my treasures. And inside my jacket, inside this pocket with a zipper that I sewed on myself, I have this very special treasure for you. I would be honored if you'd accept this earring that I found on a walk in the lot at the corner after all the pumpkins were sold last month and it was just a field again. I think it matches your ear well."

"Why, thank you. It's truly exquisite. Can you tell me more about your treasures?"

"I can. But that's probably enough for today, because I need to start cleaning now. And maybe that'll be another hundred dollars."

6

Interview with TaleSmith

"I READ THE BRIEF PARAGRAPH YOU SENT along with your request for this interview. I have it here with me. Do you mind … if I read it out loud, while the recorder is going?"

The interviewer had no problem with that and nodded her assent. The subject had her eyes down on the piece of paper in front of her, made no eye contact with her.

"Okay. 'You've been recommended by a friend, acquaintance, colleague, boss, or someone else in your life who thought you might be a good choice as a participant in my study. The study is funded by a private foundation that wishes to remain anonymous. I'm able to pay you an honorarium of one hundred dollars to be a participant. I can't tell you much about the study, other than I will record what you say, and that I want you not to use your real name, but rather a fictitious name, and because Smith is the most prevalent name in the U.S., England, and

Australia, I would like you to pick a name that has Smith in it. That's really all I can say, but I hope you'll find the opportunity enjoyable and tell me about you.'"

Silence. Fifteen seconds, thirty seconds, more. The interviewer watched the subject, whose eyes were still down, even though the paper had been removed from the table and put back in her purse.

"Okay. Am I to believe that you'd like me to come up with a make-believe name?"

The interviewer nodded.

"Then this whole thing could be made up for all you know. Every word out of my mouth could be a fairy tale."

The interviewer nodded.

"Okay. Let's call me FairySmith. For now. Maybe I'll change it later. Maybe I'll change it a few times. Then you want me to tell you about me. I can't really do that. I forget most about me, have lost me along the way, so what if I just make up a fairy tale, that may or may not be about me and people I have known?"

The interviewer nodded. The woman's eyes were still facing downward at a forty-five-degree angle directed at the middle of the round table where the digital record sat.

"Do I start with 'Once upon a time'? Isn't that how most fairy tales begin? Some generic sense of time so you don't know whether it happened yesterday or seven hundred years ago? Well, I'll try to make it clear in my tale when it began. John F. Kennedy was president, so that gives you a range of years to begin with. He died in Dallas on the day this tale began. About the time the bullets were sprayed from the window of the repository or the grassy knoll or any one of a hundred other possible locations, a woman in the woods was screaming for her life. With a husband out chopping wood in a forest behind a small cabin with a fire and a kettle of steaming hot water, the woman squirted out a little baby, red and crying and covered in goo. They named that baby … hmm … what shall her name be … let's just call her Smith, plain old Smith, because she was just a plain old baby like all the other babies born to families on that auspicious day, and pretty much every other day. Is this what you wanted from me? Does this work for you? Me telling a fairy tale instead of talking about me?"

The interviewer nodded, jotted down a few notes in her journal, kept her eyes looking at the woman, who still hadn't made eye contact with her.

"Good. Because I like fairy tales. The little girl who was born in the woods the day a president was assassinated also liked fairy tales, mostly told to her by her mother because the father was never around, always out cutting down the forest to make a pathway to town so at some point one or more of them could escape, because God knows there was need for escape. Just like Lee Harvey Oswald tried to escape. Just like Jackie tried to escape out of the backseat when she saw what was happening. Or so the little girl was told by her mother later, because she was too young to know then what was happening the day she was born. The mother taught her much about the world, the world away from their small little cabin hidden away in the woods, and she always told them with a little more light than the girl imagined existed in the real world, always told everything in fairy tale form, so there was a swaying lilt to her voice, an injection of happiness just to be telling the story even if the stories didn't have happy endings, even if the stories scared the little girl somewhat. But the mother would always end every fairy tale with a smile on her face even if it seemed inappropriate to do so …

"I could tell you the parts about big bad wolves in the woods at Grandmother's house, of which there were many, even if there was no grandmother. And I could tell you about being locked away, in towers, or dungeons, when the girl's hair grew so long and tangled she tripped over it with every step. Or about the giant bean plants outside the window before the entrance to the forest, with what the girl liked to pretend were magic beans that could take her to golden lands. Or maybe about the unhappy girl who tried to plant a garden.

"But I won't bother you with those chapters of this girl's fairy tale, because there are more chapters, like the one about the father who was supposedly chopping down trees to make a pathway for someone's escape, which turned out to be another tall tale, as the mother told the girl after she went searching for the entry point, and discovered that the father was never blazing a trail through those woods, but instead was chopping down those trees, making planks out of them, crisscrossing the planks together in a very high fence that would keep the mother and girl locked inside the father's little slice of the forest and little mess of a cabin probably forever, or at least for the rest of their lives.

"That's when the mother lost the lilt in her stories, forgot to put in the happy parts, and it seemed to the girl, who was five or seven by this point in the story, that the mother was no longer telling the stories to the little girl, but instead was telling them to herself, or some other person who wasn't in the room, who didn't seem to be listening, because the mother never looked at her anymore, was almost afraid to look in the little girl's eyes, it seemed to the little girl, and that's when the little girl began avoiding her mother's eyes as well, for fear of what she might see there, or what might not be there. It was about this time the little girl knew her mother was not going to find the pathway out of the forest that would lead them to safety in town.

"And that she was now on her own. It would be her task to save them both, to relocate in a big city like Dallas, no, not that one, never that one, bad things happen there, even worse things than happen in her father's part of the forest behind tall fences. So she went out to pick the beans to help make the father's dinner, because the mother just sat staring most days and nights out the windows, and when the father grumbled, 'What do you think you're doing?' the girl smiled, even though she was frowning inside, and told him the fairy tale about the giant and the beans and the gold and how she was going to find them fame and fortune in those beans. And the father snarled and said, 'Just cook the damn beans, in a big pot, with a glob of bacon grease and goose meat.' And she did, and she delivered it to him in a big bowl at the table and took a smaller bowl over to the seat by the window and tried to spoon feed the mother who spit the beans on the floor and mumbled about light and bullets and pathways to heaven.

"It was on the forays to the ever-growing bean plants that she was able to explore, to search for possibilities, now that the father approved of her ventures, because he truly loved her bean stew with bacon grease and goose. She would walk all along the tall fence that enclosed the whole area, circular, with no gate, because the father was big enough and strong enough to climb the fence and leap over when he needed out. And it was along these walks that she discovered the berries she knew not to eat because of the fairy tales with the poison berries her mother used to tell her when she was still able to recite and make eye contact. I feel like I'm just rambling on here, but I'm getting to the good part now, so is it okay if I just keep on talking?"

The interviewer nodded her head emphatically at the top of the woman's downward-looking head.

"So the little girl put a second towel down in her bean-collecting basket, beneath the towel that caught the beans, where she would pluck the poison berries, careful not to lick her hands and to wash carefully when she returned to the cabin. By spring, she had gathered almost a gallon of the berries that she hid underneath her bed wrapped up in the towel. Finally one day, she discovered a family of gophers behind some bean plants and berry bushes that had figured out how to move from outside the fence to inside the fence. They had dug a small hole under the fence, and her eyes got big. She looked around for the father and heard him in the distancc chopping down more trees, so she got down on her knees, skin to dirt, and thrust her nails into the loose dirt and widened the hole. But it was getting dark and she had to get back to fix his supper.

"When he sat down at the table, she noticed that he noticed something different in the stew. So she said, 'Because it's your birthday today I thought I'd make you a special stew with the raspberries from the plants down by the spring.' And he nodded, not quite smiled, but looked like he appreciated the new flavor, and took big bites, and finally lifted the bowl and drank the whole thing until the last drop slid onto his tongue. Within minutes he was holding his stomach, vomiting on the floor, falling to the ground in pain, until he stopped breathing."

She stopped, raised her eyes to meet the interviewer. "Is this what you had in mind?"

The interviewer nodded.

"Okay. Let's call me TaleSmith. I can tell these stories all night long."

7

INTERVIEW WITH
TECHSMITH

"EASY. TECHSMITH."

The interviewer waited. A half minute. A minute. TechSmith stared at her, lips tight. This one would require more interaction. Maybe he'd get rolling after the first prompt. "Can you tell me about you?"

"Me. What about me?"

She scribbled a note in the journal: *TechSmith will take some mining.*

"About your work. What defines you? What makes you tick?" She had said more than she planned.

"What defines me? What a joke. Nobody defines me. Unless you go into dictionary.com and look up the definition of 'human' and get 'of, pertaining to, characteristic of, or having the nature of people.' Does that define me? Not much of a definition, is it?

A bit circular in my opinion. Defining humans using the word 'people.' Nothing really defines me. Nobody really knows me."

Silence again. She waited longer this time. Hoped he would feel the need to fill the awkward quiet between them, doodled in her notebook, gears and triangles and other things that tech brought to mind.

Finally she said, "Why TechSmith? Can you tell me about your work?"

"TechSmith defines who I am, that's why. No. I can't tell you about my work. Top secret. I'd have to have you removed if I told you what I really do, who I really am. You don't want that, do you? Don't want to be removed, do you?"

More silence. She was losing interest in this one, first time that had happened. "Can you tell me what you do for fun?"

"Fun? You think I have fun? Maybe I do, but it's not the kind of fun you want to hear about. What do you do for fun? Do you think we could have fun together?"

She leaned in toward the recorder: "Interview with TechSmith terminated."

8

INTERVIEW WITH JILLSMITH

"I DON'T KNOW HOW TO ANSWER THE QUESTION, doesn't make sense to me. Smith? You mean pick some famous Smith and pretend I'm one of them? Like Will Smith? But he's like black and tall and a man, and I'm like the opposite of all those things. I don't know if I know any other Smiths. There's probably one on every block but I don't know any of them. Oh, how about Anna Nicole Smith? No, absolutely not. She was kind of a ditz, and I'm not, and she had watermelon breasts, and mine are more like pears or peaches. And she died way too young and I don't plan on ever dying. I'm originally from St. Louis and I think there was some famous baseball player there who was a Smith, but I only went to one game and we were drinking way too much of that expensive beer and I couldn't even tell you who won the game much less the first name of some guy whose last name might have been Smith.

"Who else? Smith. Smith. Smith. Oh yeah. How about that *Charlie's Angels* chick: Jackie Smith? Something like that. No! Jaclyn Smith. That's it. That was her. I think she was Kelly. I only know 'cause of the reruns on late-night TV. I spend a lot of time watching reruns at night when I can't sleep. Get up and make me a bag of popcorn, get a big bottle of Diet Doctor Pepper, snuggle up under a blanket with my cat, Lisette, and we watch all kinds of programs. I like the old *To Tell the Truth*s and *What's My Line?* The black-and-white thing is kind of cool. All retro and stuff. I guess I could be her. But wait. Wasn't she married like eight times? I don't want to go through all those divorces. I just want one husband 'til death do us part,' as they say, and I'm not having much luck with finding one let alone a half dozen right now so let Jaclyn Smith and Mickey Rooney keep that polygamy thing to themselves.

"Who else? I like the band the Smiths, but I don't think any of them are really named Smith, and aren't they Brits anyway? I always get the lead singer mixed up. It's not Van Morrison, and it's not Jim Morrison. But something like that. Wait. I remember I figured out a way to remember. There's this street in this town I used to live on in California and the post office was on the street that was the same name as this guy, this lead singer of the Smiths. Broadway. No, dummy. It starts with an 'M,' like the guy who played the doctor on the TV show. Morrissey. That's it. Morrissey is the Smith guy, just the one name, but he's not a Smith anyway and isn't this thing you're doing, whatever it is you're doing, about Smiths in America, not Brits? Smith. Smith.

"I remember watching some huge woman singing at sporting events when I was a kid and my parents always used to watch her and tell me to listen to the amazing voice of … what was her name … blank blank Smith … blank Smith … no, blank blank Smith. Two syllables. Da da Smith. Da da Smith. Oh, say can you see … Can't remember. Oh, wait. Jessie. Jessie Smith. No but that's close. Let me do the alphabet thing. Bessie Smith. Wait! That's it. It's Bessie Smith. Wow, it's cool when you do the alphabet thing and the second letter in the alphabet gives you the trigger. But she was big, I mean very big, and I, as you can see, am a petite little thing, as my grandma used to say when she was trying to buy me clothes for birthdays and Christmas. So, I don't think I want to be Bessie Smith either.

"I kind of like Will Smith's kids and wife. Jada is pretty cool. I like that she says, or at least somebody says, on one of those E-programs or magazines, that Jada is bisexual. Not that I am or would ever think about being or would ever have any sexual interest in another woman, but I think it's cool that some women can handle that and be so together that they could fall in love with one hundred percent of the world instead of just fifty percent of the world, so I think that's pretty cool of her to say that out loud or to say it to someone else who said it out loud, to get out of that closet while the getting is good. I like the son, Jaden, too, thought he was good in that *Karate Kid* sequel, but if I had to be one of the Smiths in that family, it should probably be Willow 'cause she's young and innocent and so am I, which is why I haven't found that death-do-us-part husband yet 'cause most guys I know aren't so innocent. Maybe I should think about becoming bisexual, find a death-do-us-part woman who's as innocent as me. No that's crazy. Wouldn't my mom just die. And Dad would disown me. But still, if I had to be a black Smith, oh, that's funny, a blacksmith, get it? If I had to be one of the black people in Will Smith's family it would be Willow … or maybe Jada … or maybe even Jaden … but definitely not Will, because we all know he is *not* innocent. He is a lady's man, and so they say, also a man's man. So not him. Not that Smith. Do I really have to be one of those famous Smiths?"

The interviewer shook her head no.

"Oh, what do you mean? I thought you said pick a Smith name. Didn't you say that? Pick a Smith name for this interview so you don't have to use my real name, so you can hide my identity in case I say anything I shouldn't be saying about somebody who might get mad and come after me if they know my real name, so I should pretend to be Jessie, or Bessie Smith or one of Will's kids? Didn't you say that?"

"No. Any Smith will do. Doesn't need to be somebody famous."

"Oh, I get it now. Doesn't have to be someone famous. Could be Fred Smith who might live across the street from me. Wait! I see the name flashing in big gold letters on the scoreboard while this guy in the Cardinals uniform does three backflips in a row, and they have a video of him on the big screen with his name flashing every time he does a backflip … Ozzie! Ozzie! Ozzie. Even though I was smashed I remember seeing that. Ozzie Smith, he was the shortstop. I liked him, liked watching him just standing there and all of a sudden flip over like a Mexican jumping bean, except he was black, too, and I'm not, and I think I should be a Smith that is most like me.

"So why don't you just call me SarahSmith, because Sarah was my mom's name and I'm probably more like her than anyone else in the world because we are both kind of innocent and trusting and it took her a very long time to find my dad and become his wife, to make him her husband, not until she was thirty-five and they conceived me very quickly after they found each other, and that's what I expect will happen to me, that I will meet Mr. Death-do-us-part and we will fall in love boom, just like that, and will have babies in a hurry, enough babies to fill up all the rooms in our very large house on a cul-de-sac on a street lined with maple and birch trees in a city that has no crime and a baseball team. And you know what else? I may very well marry a man whose last name is Smith, so calling me SarahSmith might very well be half right in the long run, and if I find Mr. Right and he doesn't like my given name I may just decide to change my name to Sarah just like my mom and I would be SarahSmith, Jr., or the second.

"Wait. That doesn't make any sense at all. But that's okay. At least I'm thinking. I'm thinking about what it would be like to be married to the same man for life and thinking about what it would be like to be called Sarah like my mom, and also thinking about what it would be like to have Smith as a last name, because you want it for me, and maybe I should want it for myself. No. How about if you just call me SarahSmith for the sake of this interview and not your study, 'cause I don't want my mom's name to show up in a study if she doesn't know about the study and doesn't know I used her name. She might not be happy about that, so I think I won't call myself SarahSmith, instead I'll be, oh I don't know. Here, let me open up the phone book, run my finger down the page, point, find the first female name. Jill. JillSmith it is. I'm kind of liking the sound of JillSmith, as opposed to WillSmith. I was getting used to being thought of as WillSmith, or having readers thinking of me as WillSmith. But if I'm looking for a death-do-us-part husband, I think JillSmith has a much sweeter and innocent sound to it. Yeah, I can get used to that. Though I could have been happy with BessieSmith if I had to.

"What I do know, for absolute certain, is that I can't and won't be called Smith with a number. Like EightSmith. I do not like the number eight at all. I was the eighth child in my family, and even though I was kind of spoiled rotten, I always had to fight to get a word in, which may be why I kind of talk now without periods. I wouldn't be able to concentrate during our interview if I thought you were writing down EightSmith in your notebook, or even just thinking of me as Smith Number Eight. I'd know it. I'd know you were thinking it and I would freeze up and not be able to speak a word. All I would be thinking about would be eight-word sentences and phrases. I'd be trying to make everything fit to eight like if I said, 'Oh, what an innocent girl I am,' I'd have to chop off the 'Oh' so it would only be eight syllables. Do you see how it works? You understand why eight is problematic? EightSmith might be a perfectly good name for somebody, for one of your subjects I'm sure, but not for me. I can't even walk into that octagon museum downtown."

The interviewer cleared her throat and spoke. "JillSmith it is."

She turned off the recorder.

9

INTERVIEW WITH ROADSMITH

"NINTH, HUH? I'd sure like to know more about the first eight. Can you tell me about who my competition is?"

The interviewer shook her head. She wanted to say they weren't his competition, more like collaborators, but she didn't want to influence his train of thought. So she kept quiet, was getting better at doing so, wrote in her notebook instead — small doodles of hedges and graffiti art she had seen on the drive here.

"What are you writing about me? Good stuff? Can I take a look? I know. I'm just messing with you. I know your study has to follow specific controls. I'll behave now. And I know you need the name. I was thinking 'TravelSmith,' but it sounds a little too much like the name of an agency that sells trips on cruise liners to Alaska or the Bahamas, and that definitely is not me. Could you imagine me stuck behind a cramped little desk in an office with venetian blinds, squeezed into a suit and tie, black leather shoes, answering phones, making cold calls? Not a chance. So we'll skip the TravelSmith.

"Then I was thinking 'WanderSmith' might be better. That's really closer to what I do, wander the planet looking for something new. Maybe I shouldn't say planet, now that I've reserved my ticket for one of the private space launches coming up in the future; I should probably make that plural, planets. Although after that one crashed last week, I'm having some second thoughts, but what the hell. I don't have the moon on my passport yet. I wonder if they'll have stamps for all the planets once private space travel is as common as riding the subway. The problem with 'wander' is that the verb falls short of what it is I actually do. Wander suggests somewhat of a willy-nilly quality, and that's not who I am. I do like a little adventure, even a modicum of danger when the rewards are worthy, but I do not wander without plan. My destinations are generally intentional, my itinerary mostly planned, my annual program usually prepared at least a year in advance. WanderSmith also sounds too similar to wanderlust, and while the lust part more accurately describes what I do, it just isn't the right fit. No, I've decided that what I do is more about being on the road, hitting the proverbial road, so you can refer to me in your study as RoadSmith. Now what?"

While the interviewer preferred the promptless recordings, inhabited only by the voice of her subjects, there were subjects who wouldn't move forward without the prompt, wanted to interview her, have a conversation, collaborate. She decided to provide the prompt this time, but turned off the recorder first before speaking, so her voice would be absent.

"Tell me about you."

"Okay, then. That's pretty broad. Tell you about me. I was an army brat. Lived in twelve different cities by the time I graduated high school; ten different schools. Because I was transient — my family, that is — so were my friendships, relationships, feelings of attachment. Not that I was antisocial or shy, you can see that's not me. I am my father's son. He was the life of every party in every town we lived in, every social event we attended, and we attended them all. And I was his son, and I adored him, wanted to be just like him. He was the original RoadSmith, so I guess we should modify my name here to RoadSmith, Jr. I've lived in Arizona, California, Colorado, Florida, Georgia, Maryland, North Carolina, Texas, Virginia, and Washington. Notice how I alphabetized them. That's something you pick up being the child of a military man, or woman. Developing systems of organization that make you efficient, sleek, ready to move.

"There's this article written by Debbie Adams, one of us, and she says, 'We are not defined by ethnicity, religion, geography, or race. You cannot spot us in a crowd. But we, the children of warriors, have been shaped by a culture so powerful we are forever different, forever proud, and forever linked to one another.' And I agree. That's all true, and we feel that unwritten connection with other kids in the DoD schools, a bond cemented in place by the professions of our fathers or mothers that brings us together. But for me we're like cars on a train. We're linked together for one ride down a track between two destinations, then we're uncoupled and hitched to another train. So, even though you establish this deep, hidden bond with folks, truly connect while you're with them, you know how to disengage, move on, live the transient lifestyle, don't get ruled by emotions. You have a logical, sensible approach to life and don't allow yourself to get derailed by being too connected to others.

"Me, I'm forever transient, always on the move. I got good at it. Dad would walk in one day, and Mom and I would stand at attention, not actually salute him, which would have been taking it a little too far, and he'd say, 'We're leaving on Tuesday. Let's get ready.' And we knew what that meant, and we'd snap into action without him having to ask twice. Mom would pull the suitcases out of the attic and begin to pack his and her clothes and shoes. The furniture was never a problem, never ours, always the same drab couches and lamps and Formica dinner tables, same on every base, would be the same in the next city, Fort Benning in Columbus, Georgia, Fort Lewis outside of Tacoma, Washington, all the same, furniture belonging to the U.S. government, on temporary loan to families like mine. I'd sometimes sit on one of those couches and wonder about the hundreds or thousands of other children of military personnel who had sat there before me, who would sit there after me.

"I had two suitcases, always readily available right under the front edge of the bed: one for my clothes, the other for whatever memorabilia I'd collected in my ten or twelve or fourteen years. I couldn't collect much. I had to prioritize, organize, had so many square inches available to me within the walls of suitcase number two to contain everything that was important to me, ready to cram it full on a minute's notice. My Willies baseball-card collection: Willie Stargell, Willie Mays, and Willie McCovey. They didn't take up much room and meant a lot to me, because my dad gave them to me on birthdays, birthdays where we had packed up everything and stuck a candle in a piece of pie in a diner on the road to celebrate my passage of time. A couple of books, a couple of journals, a handful of trinkets, things given to me by friends, by girlfriends. But those would usually disappear. Dad would come in to inspect my two suitcases before we loaded them into the car, order me to open one at a time, have me remove one piece at a time. Suitcase number one never presented a problem, clothes neatly folded, orderly, clean, but when we'd got to suitcase number two there would always be a problem — a 'cleaning of house,' as he used to put it. I'd pull out a journal and hand it to him. He'd read a couple of entries and if he didn't like what he saw he'd drop it in the trash can. I learned to write in code, not say anything that suggested I'd established close friendships or emotions unbecoming to the son of a soldier. I wrote short sentences or phrases, military in nature, brief, to the point, just stating the facts.

"As I got older and learned how to play the game, he'd let me keep the journals, make suggestions about how I might organize entries differently to save space and ink. If I held out something a friend had given me to remember them by, like the small drawing in pencil a girl at Fort Bliss outside of El Paso gave me the day we left Texas, along with a little kiss on my cheek? That drawing was crumpled and dropped in the trash can, and pretty much the memory of the kiss along with it.

"Then we'd be on the road: ready for our new life, new home, new set of acquaintances to make, new cities and forts to explore. Fort Lee, Fort Bragg, Fort Carson, Camp Blanding. I've got a whole journal full of them. Full of factual information about each. No memories, no emotional drivel, as dad would say. Population, altitude, commanding officers, other pertinent and relevant information befitting the son of an army man. So, rather than drive myself crazy — which happened to a lot of the other RoadSmiths — I learned to accept it, even to like it, to look forward to it. It was like a gift; a sense of anticipation grew.

"Dad would drop a hint at dinner one night. 'We'll be having a family meeting in the morning: 0600.' I could hardly keep my feet still under the table, and barely got an hour's sleep imagining where we might end up geographically before the week was out. It wasn't that I got bored with any of the places we were stationed. More that I would research and study and learn everything about a place within the first six months, and after that I'd find myself getting attached to the people more than I should. Because I knew what was coming, I'd be ready to leave, ready to detach myself from Thompson or Scully or Williams. That's another thing we brats tended to do — still do. Use last names. Use the surnames of our fathers or mothers to address each other. I never got over it. It became me. Made me who I am today.

"I bounced around to five different colleges before graduating. Never married. No kids. Lots of girlfriends scattered all over the world. I hope you don't get the wrong impression of me. I'm not a womanizer. I'm just a RoadSmith and have no time to settle down and establish a normal relationship with a wife and kids, dog and cat, a house that needs new paint every seven years. That's not me. I just can't live that way. And there are lots of us like that out there. A lot of my friends, girlfriends, also grew up in the military and have similar values, or faults you might call them. Or deficiencies. I just call them adaptations. Making the best of the values that have been ingrained into our DNA.

"That's why my work now takes me all over the world as I guide small groups of highly interested travelers to exotic locations. They pay well, and I actually have a savings account now. Next month I'm taking a group of ten on a month-long trip to Hawaii. I call it the Volcanic Voyage, where we'll visit the three active Hawaiian volcanoes. Two months after that I'll be doing African Waterfalls, then Brazil by Boat, and end the year with a Peace Pact to Israel and Palestine. That's why you can call me the RoadSmith."

10

INTERVIEW WITH MINDSMITH

THE INTERVIEWER LOOKED AT HER WATCH as the subject walked in the room, plopped a backpack on the floor and himself in the chair. She turned on the recorder before he could catch his breath.

"I'm so sorry I'm late. I'm never late, to a fault. I can't stand when other folks are late, so I'm always fifteen minutes early. Is this thing on?"

The interviewer nodded, wrote in her journal.

"Will I get docked for being late? I'm so sorry."

"No docking."

"Again, so sorry. I have just had the day from hell, something penned by Dante on a bad day. But you don't want to hear about this stuff, do you?"

"Yes, it's perfect. Go for it." She didn't want to slow him down and remind him about establishing his Smith name, he was so jacked up, and she wanted him like this.

"I have to go all the way back to three thirty-three this morning, which is the time I woke up according to the digital clock at the foot of the bed that tells me so in large orange numbers every morning. I prefer to wake up closer to five so I have a full six or seven hours in. And those six or seven hours are usually good ones, because I sleep soundly. Five and a half is cutting it a bit short, but I can tell it's over with, I'm awake, so I get up, pee, take a big drink of water in case I had any dreams last night that want to be remembered, which is what I do with the water thing, then sit in my chair at the foot of the bed, my comfortable easy chair from Macy's in San Jose, with my Herman Miller computer desk and MacBook Pro waiting for me.

"I pop the lid and leave the screen on low energy to limit the amount of light in the room so my wife can continue in what sounds like a deep and comfortable sleep, wishing I was there with her. I'm playing my Words with Friends game, I have five of them going, and in every game my opponent has played a seven-letter word and has taken the lead. I mean, I love it when anyone finds a seven-letter play, but for all five to have found them at the same time is a little bit absurd, and I chuckle, a little sardonically, and hear my wife respond in her sleep with a friendly grunt.

"While in Facebook, which is where I play my WWF and Scrabble games, I check the latest headlines to see that Russia has decided to conduct patrol missions over the Gulf of Mexico and it makes me sick to my stomach because there are enough other reasons right now to think the end of the world is coming like global warming and the lack of rain on the West Coast and volcanoes rumbling everywhere and swarms of earthquakes popping up all over the planet. Then I read the headline about Thich Nhat Hanh who has just had a brain hemorrhage at the age of eighty-eight and I imagine at that age he won't survive it well and will probably die soon. Then I see a tagline about an interview in 2012 where he says humans shouldn't worry about their coming extinction, and I read on, and he talks about the global warming of the past where a six-centigrade increase wiped out the whole planet, ninety-five percent of all species, and it's been happening cyclically for three hundred and fifty million years, and that in this global warming cycle ninety-five percent of life, including homo sapiens, will become extinct again, and will be replaced by something else.

"And while I'm reading the headline that the Warriors lost to the San Antonio Spurs, every electronic device in the bedroom begins to whir and spin and blink, my wife's phone bouncing up and down on her nightstand, the cable box flashing the latest time, three fifty-five, both printers in the room flashing and blinking and whining, only my computer stays on because it doesn't need electricity given its overnight charge, still at one hundred percent, as a huge white light flashes out the window and I think about Russian nuclear bombs aboard planes floating over the Gulf of Mexico and extinction and remember that the transformers up Rodeo Gulch Road blow up at least once a year in winter.

"I'm sitting in total darkness except for the light of my computer screen and I think I should probably get some NaNoWriMo writing in now that Comcast is down and along with it the internet so I can't finish my word games, and I stare at the blinking cursor wondering who the interviewer will interview today, with no ideas emerging, and the power comes back, with a reversal of gold and yellow and blue lights with whining and whirring and the revving of engines in both printers and my wife's iPhone. These practice attempts at the end of the world occur two more times before the power decides to stay, four outages altogether, each with a cracking flash of light filling the sky outside the bedroom window, and I choose to think of it as the fireworks display over Lake Merritt in Oakland when I was maybe ten years old, the whole sky bright with light, like downtown Las Vegas lit with the marquees of dozens of casinos.

"With the power and internet back I play 'gestalt' and 'afar' and 'bonging' and 'quin,' feeble attempts at trying to catch up to my worthy opponents. When the light of dawn begins to break through outside my window, I resume my NaNoWriMo writing, slipping into an interview that eventually works up to speed as the subject finds his or her voice and takes control over the fingers typing on my keyboard.

"My wife is up by now, the multiple power surges effectively eliminating any further hope of sleep, on her second large cup of caffeinated coffee, and she brings me my standard breakfast: two pieces of what we call prison bread, Dave's bread in the yellow wrapper, Dave, who spent time in prison and decided to change his life by making his dad's old bread recipes when he got out, with all the seeds inside and out, covered with super chunky Skippy peanut butter, and a sixteen-ounce bottle of Calistoga to wash it all down. And it's six thirty now and here comes the best part of the day: when I decide to get back into bed and so does my wife and we get naked and start the day right with mutual orgasms.

"Let me clarify. By mutual I don't mean that we have them at the same time, which doesn't happen much for us at age sixty-four and almost sixty-four in a couple of weeks, but what I mean is that we both have them, both help each other achieve them, and they are good, always good, but exceptionally good at seven in the morning. But Larry will be here to pick me up at seven thirty so we can go to Techshop, and I have prep to do: files to transfer to my flash drive, materials to gather, and the biggest task, coverboard to cut into twenty-four-by-eighteen-inch sheets that will fit in the laser cutter.

"When I get to the workshop to get two sheets of coverboard, the stack is completely covered with stuff, I won't say with shit—which is what I felt like saying at the time — because it was reams of paper, and pads of bamboo paper for making signatures, and other … okay, other shit, because for me to pull two sheets out, I have to bend over, get down on the ground on my knees, with two knees that don't work anymore and two hips that are being ground down because the knees don't work anymore, and I'm in pain. So I pull everything out, scatter it on the couch and the worktables and the floor until I reach the two sheets of coverboard and slice them up. Larry is early and I'm late and the slicing takes a while, but I finally get my Techshop bag packed with four sheets of coverboard, a small sheet of cherry wood, some butt board to cut sheets for Stuart's gameboard, some baby wipes, cutters, empty plastic bags for finished pieces, my book full of technical notes, and a bottle of water.

"The trip from Santa Cruz to San Jose on Highway 17 is smooth and uneventful, as Lance and I catch up about movies and sports and projects we're working on. Everything goes well at Techshop — me working on the laser cutter from nine to eleven, and while Lance continues working until twelve, I go sit out in the lobby and work a little more on my NaNoWriMo, getting about three hundred words done, which is another good part of the day, because I'm following through with my monthlong commitment, with approximately twenty-five thousand words already on day twelve when the official goal is fifty thousand, my unofficial goal being closer to sixty-five thousand, which will give me approximately two hundred twenty pages.

"We order our favorite lunches of the week at the Gyro truck — lamb gyros with tomatoes, onions, lettuce, a great sauce, and the best wraps I've ever tasted. Back at home before one, I work on the crossword puzzle and have trouble with the last few clues, don't know 'sleeping giant or gargantuan,' and give up and take a nap, another good part of the day when I can actually fall asleep and rest in daylight.

"I forgot to mention the two bags of popcorn I had at Techshop, because they have a popcorn maker in the lobby, and members can have as much free popcorn as they want, and I wanted two bags full this morning, and this is important because it probably comes into play a little later in the evening.

"After dinner, my wife reminds me that I have to get gas before I head out to my Wednesday night writers' salon group across town. So I get dressed, pack my computer, a bottle of water, and turn on my car with the gas light blinking at me: feed me, feed me, feed me please, or I will stop on the side of a dark road in the middle of the night on your way home with nobody to help you, and you will have to walk to a gas station and find a gas can, and fill it up and walk back to your car, or call AAA and wait two hours before they get to you, so please fill me up, now, right now.

"So I do. I drive to the Union station at the corner by the freeway and open my gas tank and put the nozzle in and give the machine my zip code and push the catch on the nozzle so the 10.5 gallons will automatically fill my tank while I go inside and get something sweet to eat. I find Pepperidge Farm Chessmen, which I love, because they are the closest thing to shortbread that a Quik Stop-type service station store has, and there's a line of people, and it takes time, and I'm thinking about Techshop and NaNoWriMo and the big poetry event tomorrow, and when I finally get to the counter I'm thinking about the absurd amount of makeup on the clerk who helps me, wondering about why someone would want to hide themselves like that, and I walk out to my car, driver's-side door facing me, and I get in, and I drive away, feeling a little bump, probably one of those metal plates in the pavement and I head over toward the exit to get on the freeway and see someone running at my car in the mirror and I slow down, but I'm a little concerned about his intentions so I continue to move toward the on-ramp and he yells at me so I stop again. 'You'd better stop,' he says. 'You've got a nozzle hanging out of your gas tank.'

"I get out of the car to look, and there is not only the nozzle from the pump still sticking out of my car, but the whole ten feet of hose connected to the nozzle, dragging on the ground next to my car, and I'm a little bit in shock, trying to figure out what the hell just happened, and I'm thinking if the nozzle and hose is dangling from my car, what about the gas, is it spewing out of the pump into the gas station and will the whole place and me and my car soon catch fire and blow up. An attendant tells me I have to come back and pay for what I've done, and I'm thinking thousands of dollars and will I have to replace the gas pump and how insane this is, and I'm not really embarrassed because I'm still a little bit in shock, and trying to figure out how I forgot to take the nozzle out, and it must have been the damn chessmen, anticipation of the crunchy shortbread in my mouth, feeding my sugar craving. After the attendant walks me over to the gas pump, puts the nozzle back in the holder, analyzes the hose, shows me the metal valve that was broken off at the pump, he tells me to go inside and pay.

"I go inside and there are five people in line, and as I'm standing there waiting, another two people get in line behind me, and I let them go in front of me because I don't want anybody in there to hear the story of how I wrecked one of their gas pumps, and finally I'm alone with the clerk, and she doesn't exhibit any shock or surprise about my bozo move, as if it happens every day, and she says, 'The hose is okay, so the valve is a hundred dollars.' It's as if they stock valves on the shelf next to the Pepperidge Farm cookies, a valve that maybe they pay seventy-five dollars for so they get their thirty-percent mark-up, but I don't care, think a hundred dollars is a deal for what I just did, and she continues, 'You can pay for this with a credit card, or you can fill out paperwork and file an insurance claim.' And I hand her my credit card, gladly, the same card I just used to put thirty-one dollars and fifteen cents' worth of gas in my car, and she tells me it's denied. And I tell her to try it again because it's fine and it's denied again. I swipe it two more times and it is denied two more times. I finally give her my JoKa Press card, because I have no money in my money clip, and it's currently my only option, unless I want to stand there and fill out paperwork for an insurance claim, and now I'm close to being late for my writers' salon, which I don't like to do, because I'm never late, and I like to get my good chair.

"Back at the car, the madness nearly behind me, I turn on the engine and see flashing at me: *You need maintenance soon.* Isn't that the truth. When I finally get to my writers' salon and sit in my good chair, I feel my bowels rumbling and I have to squeeze my butt cheeks to make it to the bathroom, which is only about five feet away from the living room where we meet and write, and I close the door, barely make it to the toilet seat, and I explode, a few times, and I know they're waiting for me to get started, and what I have just exploded has a rancid odor, and yes, I know I need maintenance, and I open the window, and wash my hands with way too much soap because I want the odor of the soap to overtake the odor I've left behind, and finally make it back out to the room, feeling like Kilauea in Hawaii, always rumbling, always ready to blow. I guess you can call me MindSmith, as in I must be losing mine."

11

INTERVIEW WITH RADIOSMITH

"Oh, I don't know nothin' 'bout no Smiths. Used to have a Nate Smith back in '75 who was a shipmate. He was the cook. He could turn a pile of sea rations into one of them there gourmet meals. Nate Smith. What a character. He was from Alabama. He was colored. We'd come into port out there in the Pacific and those folks there ain't seen many colored folks. Nate was a sweet guy. Stayed away from the poker games and dice games. Not like those other swabbies who'd be broke between one paycheck to another, one port to another. Don't know any other Smiths, though. I don't quite know what you mean."

"Well, for the purpose of our conversation, I like for my subjects to take on an anonymous name."

"I don't know what that means."

"Anonymous means that we'll call you by a name that isn't really yours. A name with Smith in it. Like the travel guide I interviewed

69

went by RoadSmith. I've had a TechSmith, a JustSmith. You're my eleventh interview. What kind of Smith would you like to be?"

"Hmm. Sounds kinda crazy to me, but I'll play along. I see you got my MacNaughton's poured, neat, just like I like. Maybe after a coupla tilts I can find a Smith in me. Maybe because I was a merchant marine for fifty-nine years, we could call me MerchantSmith. Or SailSmith. No. What I did all those years was operate the radios. Let's just call me RadioSmith. That's good. And thank you again for the MacNaughton's. What do ya want to know about me? You get a coupla MacNaughton's in me and I may be telling you stories that get a little blue. Life on that big blue ocean got a little randy at times, lots of pretty young things inhabiting all those Pacific Islands and the Orient. Is that the kinda stuff you wanta hear?"

"I want to hear anything and everything you want to tell me."

"Okay, then. I guess you want to know about what my quality of life was like living on the sea. I signed up back in 1920, on my fifteenth birthday, born in aught five. Took a ship outta San Francisco, where my family lived. Ma didn't like it, didn't like me leaving so young, but I grew up a little too fast, beyond my years, so I had to get outta there. Dad was glad to see me go, and I was glad to get as far away from that miserable cuss as I could. Sis was the one, though. She wouldn't stop crying and grabbing onto my coat sleeve and pants when we was down on the dock and I was getting ready to board. Ma finally had to grab her loose and set me free. Dad wasn't there of course, down at his restaurant cutting up meat for dinner, having himself a nip so he could see a little straighter.

"Had a little restaurant down on Maiden Lane and all his buddies came there to eat and drink into the wee hours. And when he'd get home, if I was asleep, he'd wake me up, tell me to sit up in bed, just so's he could whack me upside the head. That's why I lied about my age, 'cause I looked much older than I was, said I was eighteen, and hopped on that merchant ship fast as I could, pointed about two thousand miles west. I swabbed up lots of decks and helped in the kitchen for a coupla years, but I gotta tell you, even that was about one thousand percent better than the quality a life I had back in the city.

"Ol' Red Molson, the radio operator, first time he saw me, there was kind of a twinkle in his eye, and he recognized something in me that he liked, as did I, and he took a liking to me, as did I to him. He's the one who taught me how to drink MacNaughton's neat … don't mind if I do … ahh … Red took me under his wing so to speak and taught me everything there was to know about radios and communicating, not just the talking and the note-taking, but the mechanics of that there contraption that I knew nothing about when I was fifteen. Red died a couple years in. Caught malaria from one of those sweet little things that wasn't so sweet, and they put me on the radio at age seventeen.

"Now I'm getting the proper blend of MacNaughton's in my blood I can think a little straighter. I told you Ol' Red died of malaria, but that ain't right. He died of something else horrible and I can't quite remember what it was. We didn't get malaria out there in the Pacific. We got lots of other things like clap, an' gonorrhea, had to get lots of shots in our ass to make sure we didn't bring nothing home to our families. I didn't have no family to speak of back in the beginning, no girlfriend or wife, wasn't even twenty yet, but I did get me a wife up in Portland when we come into port back in, what was it now, let me take a swig and see if I can jog the memories.

"I think it was '26. I was twenty-one. God. Twenty-one. Can you imagine being twenty-one again? Well, hell, you ain't much older than that now. That was seventy years ago. You know I'm ninety-one now. Just last week. And I can still put down a quart a MacNaughton's a day. I met Margaret in one of those dance clubs up in Portland, in one of those downtown dives, and we danced and drank all night long, then got one of those five-dollar rooms for about three days straight while I was still on leave. Woke up Monday morning with about five empty bottles on the floor and a ring on my finger and a wife on my arm. Now I'd have to be careful. Now I had someone back home to make sure I didn't give nothing to. Except my paycheck. That was Margaret and we had two kids before she got rid of the likes of me. She could keep up with me for a while, tossing 'em back just as good as me, but she lost interest. And one year I didn't get enough shots in time, and she went to the doctor and came home and slapped me upside the head with a tire iron she brought out of her trunk and told me to get the hell out, and I did.

"It was my sister who stuck by me, all those years. It was her who wrote me letters every week, and I'd write back some, but I don't spell so well, so they were kinda short letters. Every port we landed in, I'd buy her something. Had a trunk in my radio room where I stored stuff for six to ten months before we'd circle back and head home. Home. That's kinda funny. I got to thinking that ship was my home, those other folks on it with me as my family. Spent more time, good times and bad times, with any of them than I did my family. But Sis was always there. Sent her lots of carved statues from the islands. Sent her one of those good-smellin' sandalwood elephants carved real nice with little ivory tusks sticking outta its head. Sent her fancy framed pictures, and kimonos when we was in Japan. She appreciated those gifts. Has 'em all over her house when I come home on leave, all spread out everywhere for me to see.

"Then I met Irene Rainwater up in Port Angeles. You can kinda get a hint from her name she was an Indian. She was nearly six feet tall and had a tongue on her wouldn't take no crap from anybody, especially an old salt like me. So we hooked up, and she didn't mind the drinking, she liked it, and she took on to MacNaughton's with me real quick. Every time I get home, she'd have a couple cases stored up so we could have a party the minute I showed up. She couldn't have no kids. Which was a good thing. Didn't have to worry about another leaving me 'cause I couldn't support her kids. Just her and me. I loved her a lot. And she understood about my life on the sea and how I'd get lonely out there and when we was in port all of us salts together we got kinda wild and drunk and sometimes partied a little more than we shoulda. But she knew all about it. Smiled at me with those eyes that twinkled, saying 'You scoundrel' but smiling all the while. So I loved that one. Wouldn't been a quality life without her. I sent her even more stuff than I sent Sis. I sent her some of those big couches with the carved mahogany all around the top and bottom and legs like the feet of a lion, sent those back from the Orient, sent four over about ten years and they are in our little apartment in the Mission District in San Francisco, which is where we live now.

"They made me retire back aways, so we moved to SF. Got us a little place in the Mission cross the street from a schoolyard so we can watch the kids coming and going every day. Yep. They made me retire at seventy-four, said I needed to live for a while on land, needed to let someone new take over the radios 'cause there was new fandangled stuff on them I didn't know nothing about, but I took that whippersnapper they sent in to replace me and I taught him a few things. More than a few things. I taught him how to tear apart them old radios and replace the bulbs and connect new wires, and, most important, I cracked open a brand spanking new bottle of MacNaughton's and taught him how to drink like a real radio operator should know how to drink. Had to wipe him up off the floor the next morning, him and what fell outta him the night before. We had a good laugh about that when I walked off that ship for the last time and started my land-worthy life in San Francisco where I spent a lot of time with my wife and my sis.

"Played lots of cards the past seventeen years. We like canasta. I especially like red threes 'cause you get a hundred points for them things. And I like it when I get those natural red canastas cause they're worth five hundred points. Down the hall here, I gotta whole room of old radios. Sent 'em home over the years and Irene never tossed a one out, saved 'em for me, kept 'em polished and neat. Just like I like my MacNaughtons."

12

INTERVIEW WITH CARDSMITH

"HOW'D YOU GET MY NAME?"

"I interviewed a friend of yours. He gave me your name. Said you play poker together."

"Oh, yeah. He gave you my name?"

"You can't say his name while we're recording. Everything is anonymous."

"I understand. What would you like to know?"

"I need you to give me a pseudonym, and I'm calling all my subjects BlankSmith, so you can think up something you'd like to use instead of Blank."

"It's CardSmith."

"Great. So tell me about you. Who is CardSmith? What makes you tick? How did a woman like you get into cards?"

"Pretty girls like you make me tick. Makes my heart beat faster. Pretty boys make me tick, too. The professor, though, he's a little more aged, like a fine wine or cheese, so there's no tick there, more of a purr. He's a master at pool. I won't play him, but I love to watch him. Something so pure and fluid about the way he strokes that cue, the way he moves around the table like I imagine a black panther would move around a herd of gazelles, waiting to strike. I am attracted to certain people, and certain people are attracted to me. I tend to find more of them in card rooms than I do elsewhere in my life. It's a good fit for me. Gambling is in my blood. My family were among the first Chinese to come to town, lived down by the river where the theater is now. Those guys could gamble. But the games they played were based on luck and they would always lose, their paychecks, their rent, their wives and kids. But they taught me how to think like a gambler, gave me the itch.

"Where they stopped short, not understanding the mathematical calculations that accompany the playing of games, I zoomed on ahead, got my first degree in applied math at Berkeley, my master's and PhD in games theory at MIT. Do you remember the movie with Kevin Spacey and his students trying to break the bank in Vegas? *21*. He was my teacher, the guy his character was based on. I was a consultant on the movie, helped them set up hands and make appropriate bets. But blackjack is only about making money. You're only playing against the house, one opponent. If I want to make some quick cash, I'll head to Tahoe or Vegas and take in a twenty-four-hour session at a twenty-five-dollar table, so as not to draw too much attention, don't want them to think, or know, that I'm a high roller, so I play under the radar, put on my dark glasses and no makeup, try to make myself plain.

"I know, you're saying, 'How can you make yourself plain with that gorgeous face and body?' But I play down. Wear a baggy sweatshirt and sweatpants and tennis shoes. Save the silk dresses and high heels for the clubs after I win a few thousand. You know Geena Davis, right? My IQ is two points above hers, so understanding the calculations in blackjack and poker is ingrained in me. I can't keep from counting the cards in blackjack and making myself the favorite over the house in the long run. It's impossible for me to not calculate the odds on my two cards plus the three on the flop in comparison with those of my opponents. This is why I play poker.

"I have opponents. Sometimes worthy opponents, which I prefer, anywhere from eight to one at a time, and this is what makes my body hum. It's not like a purr, but more of a rich, deep hum like the engine of a very expensive car. Sometimes it's my whole body; sometimes I can feel it in my fingertips; and other times it's actually in my throat, grabs hold of my vocal cords and vibrates them. It's hard to explain. You really need to feel it to understand it.

"I played poker when I was in elementary school with my brothers and dad and uncles, but they didn't know how to play. I can see the numbers and percentages floating above the cards, kind of suspended just above the table, and back then they wiggled at me and gave me clues and told me when to stay and when to fold. I always cleaned them out. They never learned. They always invited me back to the game because they wanted to win their money back, but it never happened. I kept putting their money in the bank, calculated my monthly interest, moved it around to accounts with better yields, and if I hadn't received any scholarships, I could still afford to go to Cal and MIT on my own. But of course I got scholarships, because, you know, I am kind of a genius.

"I should probably quit saying that. It's not kind of. I just am a genius. I met Geena Davis once. We hit it off well. It's not often you get to speak to someone who's able to think on the same level as you when you have IQs over one sixty, so I really enjoyed hanging out with and drinking with her. She's another one who made me purr. I helped her study for a part she was thinking of taking about a woman gambler, so we played cards and drank single malt scotch and smoked Cuban cigars somebody gave her. She's a smart, tall, attractive woman. It's hard to believe that she was married to Jeff Goldblum. Maybe he was a good lover, but the conversations must have been boring as hell.

"We had a game at Cal, me and two of my friends bought a professional poker table with my savings, real chips, an antique set from Harvey's, which they don't sell anymore. We'd buy the chips and beer and provide the weed. We'd hacked into the school's database and checked the background of our dorm mates and classmates to find out who came from money, and we'd chum up with these guys, mostly guys, occasionally women, and we'd start inviting them to the game, and they loved it. Loved playing with three hot Asian chicks, loved that they could just show up and all the food and drink and pot they wanted was there for free. But they eventually paid for it. We could've tag-teamed them and cheated, but we didn't need to. They'd get shit-faced and stoned and after they emptied their wallets and wrote us checks or promised us they'd go to the bank in the morning, they left with a smile on their faces, because they could afford to lose, were used to paying for their fun, and we were fun. And sometimes one of them would make us tick, and we'd let them spend the night and we'd drain them dry just a little more. God, I loved Berkeley.

"All three of us went to MIT together and we worked up a similar routine there, but word had spread a little bit about us, the guys there were smarter than the ones at Berkeley, and cared a little more about their money than the gold-spoon boys at Cal. We still made enough money to pay for our tuition and buy the kind of clothes we needed to make a scene in Cambridge and Boston. God, we could make a scene, make those boys drool when the three of us hit the dance floor together wearing one piece of thin clothing and some tall black heels, rubbing up against each other and everyone else on the floor. We were hot stuff, and we had fun. I am still hot stuff, as you can see. And I still have fun. Just a little bit more refined these days; a little more discriminatory, now that people recognize me more.

"When I play in tournaments there's no hiding who you are, because they're always pointing at you and some interviewer is always sticking a mic or a camera in your face and asking you inane questions, so I wear disguises these days, carry around a wardrobe full of costumes, if you will, that turn me into something other than myself. Not always glamorous, sometimes I'll dress homeless, or hooker. Or just plain Jane when I don't want to be noticed. Like in cash games where I don't know anybody. Just some Chinese chick walking in from off the street into what they think is the wrong game and they think they'll empty my pockets fast and I slice through them like Zorro. Leave them barely with pants on. That's when I'll dress plain or stupid or just ugly.

"The big games — like at the Bellagio or the Wynn — I can't hide in those games. Everybody knows me now. When I walk in, they don't point, but they give those little head nods to each other, acknowledging that I have entered the room and they'd better hold onto their Rolex watches and diamond ear studs, because you know who's in the house.

"Have you ever slept with any of your subjects, yet? You are a cutie, you know. I could teach you some things. Do you mind if I talk dirty into your recorder? So this is what makes me tick. This is what I do in a game with a bunch of guys holding their hard hands when they're playing with me. I pretend ditzy and drunk; I talk dirty and flirt with them and make them think I'm heading upstairs to the penthouse with them after the game. And then I empty their pockets, make them write IOUs, make them literally limp away from the table, a few inches shorter in every part of their bodies. I put my winnings in the club bank so I don't get mugged by some punks on the way to the elevator, then pop into the club to find some sweet young thing who doesn't emit the smell of losing but instead reminds me of me and my girls at Berkeley and MIT. If you really want to know, I am insatiable. That's probably the best descriptor of me. I can't get enough sex, enough partying, and especially enough cardplaying. Sex and partying is one thing, I stand corrected, actually two things. But I don't feel the hum there. Don't get me wrong. I am the life and star of every party, but it's mostly an act, something I'm used to playing and I play it well, so I try it on. Like a good improv. When I drink and party and fuck, I love the improv of it. But when I play cards, it's much more.

"Yes, there's a little improv there with the role-playing as I screw with my opponents' minds. And sitting at a green felt table is the only place I can feel the hum. Whether I'm winning or losing, but I rarely lose, it's there, just the thought of being there, no not the thought, just the being there and having it course through my circulatory system and take me over. That's the thing, that's my addiction. It's not so much about the two cards I'm dealt, but almost always about the psychological constructs of my opponents. Game theory was easy for me, I didn't really have to study, because it was second nature. So I took every psychology class I could and I devoured it, learned about what makes people tick, and how to read their facial tics and tapping of their fingers, and deep sighs, and when it was phony for effect.

"That's what hooks me about this game. That my aura actually taps into the auras of my opponents and, one at a time, I can ensnare them, wrap them up so they can't see straight, make them think the opposite of what they should be thinking, make them push all in when I've got the nuts, make them fold when I'm holding deuce seven offsuit. It's the mental thing that gets me off. I mean, I've actually had orgasms right there at the table when I've successfully lassoed and hog-tied an opponent who hands me every dollar they have, with a smile. I'll make a little squeal, to cover up the little orgasm, make it seem like I'm just a dumb lucky girl who doesn't know what the hell she's doing."

13

Interview with PetSmith

"I'M NOT USED TO SPEAKING OUT LOUD TO ADULTS. This might be hard for me. Talking to you, to this microphone. I usually talk to animals, and they don't talk back. Well, that's not true. They definitely communicate with me, especially when I'm taking such good care of them. Can I have a glass of water? My throat's a little dry. Like I said, talking like this doesn't come easy. Thank you.

"I guess it would have to be PetSmith. Do you have pets? That's how I know if I like people or not. If they don't have pets, I'm not sure why I would ever trust them, or would ever want to be their friend. If you can't share your life with a pet, then you must be a very selfish person. I'm not saying you're selfish. I don't even know you, and you haven't really told me if you have a pet.

"See? I'm not very good at this talking stuff. When I do have to talk, when I know this recorder is on and taking down every

81

word I say, I get a little nervous. Not a little nervous, a lot nervous. Look. I'm sweating. Feel my forehead. My parents were both very quiet people, who mostly just read in their spare time. And not out loud. Not to me. Don't get me wrong. I loved them very much, but they didn't talk to me much. They were very shy. Very reserved. Very English. I am my parents' child. Even more shy and quiet than them because I have both their genes in me. This interview is kind of like I'm talking to a pet, because you don't say anything, don't talk back to me. Maybe if you barked or purred, I'd feel a little more comfortable. I might be all talked out. I don't know if I can do this much longer. Can I have some more water? Thank you."

"Why don't you tell me about your work? You seem to like what you do?"

"That's a good idea. I can do that. For a while. You are right. I love my work. You know, when I graduated high school, I knew exactly what I wanted to be, wanted to do. I wanted to be a veterinarian, so I could work with animals. We didn't have pets in my house. My parents didn't want to have to deal with the work it took to care properly for pets. Of course they wouldn't want to have to speak to them, to show them love and affection, or to scold them. It would be like having another child, and one was enough for them, which is probably why I had no brothers and sisters. I think even one child, me, was more than they wanted to handle, which is one reason why they never really talked to me unless they had to. Can I have some more water, please? You know, the only way I'll be able to keep talking is if I think of you as a big fluffy poodle, because I love them most. Is that too weird? Is it okay if I think of you as a dog?"

"Yes, that's fine. Woof."

"That's funny. You're funny. I'll bet your pets love you. Pets like a sense of humor. I'll sometimes tell my animals jokes, little animal puns. Here's one. What happens when it rains cats and dogs? You don't have to guess. I'll just tell you. You might step in a poodle. Isn't that funny? I don't tell that one to poodles, though. They wouldn't think it was so funny to get stepped on. But I'll tell them one about cats instead, like what is a cat's favorite color? Ready? Purr-ple. I've got a bunch of these. I'm finding it much easier to talk to you imagining you as a big white French poodle, hair down over your eyes so you can't see me."

"That's great. Do you want to tell me about where you work?"

"Oh, that's right. That's what I'm supposed to talk about. When I went to community college, I couldn't do the math and science classes very well, so I couldn't get into Long Beach, and had to give up my dream of becoming a veterinarian. But I went to all the veterinarian hospitals in my area to see if I could work for them — be an assistant or something — so I could still be around animals. I don't think I would have been a good veterinarian though, because I wouldn't have been able to stick them with needles to give them their shots. It would have felt like I was shoving those needles into myself, and I hate needles. It took me a long time to find a vet that would hire me. I don't do well at the interviews. I'm too quiet. I don't answer the questions well and I get nervous. Water, please. Thank you.

"But finally, one day I went to an interview with a vet and she didn't ask me a bunch of questions. She just put me with animals and watched me with them. That's all it took. I was hired on the spot. You know, I'm surprised I'm talking so much. But you're very easy to talk to. I worked with a white poodle once, and her name was Fifi, so when I talk, I'm thinking of you as Fifi, and it's much easier to say things like I would to her. I know you wanted to hear about where I work now, but I thought I'd tell you how I got there. Fifi would want to hear that. And I've actually told her this story, so it's easier for me to talk if I remember what I said to her.

"I loved Dr. Vicki so much and I loved her veterinarian hospital, and I really liked it when she fixed sick pets and made them healthy again. But, after about three months, I couldn't take it. I hated seeing when she had to put animals down. That's the nice way of saying she had to kill them. I guess you could say euthanize, but that's no better. It's all the same. They're dead and gone, and I had to assist her with the injections, hold those poor little helpless animals as she stuck that poison into their systems and ended their lives. Dr. Vicki was kind, though. She understood and tried to keep me away from the animals she had to put down. But that was hard for her because she needed help and I couldn't help.

"One day when I was about to quit, or maybe she was about to fire me, a client came in with a Labrador that hurt its leg. The client was not the dog's owner, but his caregiver at a facility not too far away. I had never heard of such a thing, but she worked at a place called the D Pet Hotel. While she was waiting for Dr. Vicki to fix Ralph's leg, she told me about where she worked. Like always, I just listened and nodded my head as she talked. She was a talker, seemed to like to talk to strangers like me, even if I didn't talk back. She told me all about the D Pet Hotels and, when I told Dr. Vicki about them, she called up the owner and gave me a great recommendation and I was hired the following week.

"It all worked out fine. Dr. Vicki was happy she didn't have to fire me, and I was happy I didn't have to quit, and Dr. Vicki was able to hire a new assistant who could stand to watch her kill those poor suffering animals. And I was happy. Who knew there was such a thing as a pet hotel. The one I work at is in Hollywood, but they have two more: one in Scottsdale, Arizona, and another one in New York City. Would you mind if I brushed those bangs out of your eyes?"

"No, I'm fine, thanks. Would you like some more water?"

"Yes, please. But I think I need to pee first. Sorry for just saying pee rather than use the bathroom or the facilities, but that's the way we talk to our pets. They know they need to pee so that's what we say. Well, that's what I say anyway. I'll be right back."

"Okay. That's better. Do you want to hear more about the D Pet Hotels?"

"That would be great, thanks."

"I can tell you this. I love my work. It's the perfect job for me. I get to meet new pets all the time, and I get to spend time with returning pets who have become my friends, because these wealthy actors and Hollywood folks travel a lot and drop their pets off with us, which is kind of sad for the pets, that they don't get to spend enough time with their owners, but good for me, because I get to spend more time with them and establish more meaningful relationships with them.

"We have three suite sizes. Which one the owner chooses pretty much depends on how much money they can afford to spend. The Small Suite is only four feet by nine feet, and a little cramped by my standards. The Sensational Suite is better, twelve feet by twelve feet, and has a nice thirty-two-inch flat-screen TV. My favorite is the Uber Suite, because every pet deserves one. It's twelve feet by twenty-two feet, has a forty-two-inch flat-screen TV, a queen bed, and has exquisite modern decor.

"We have an interior decorator who designs and outfits all the suites for us. I get to help make decisions on colors and fabrics, because they know I have a sixth sense for understanding the needs of pets. If you don't need to have your pet spend the night in one of our suites, we also offer day care, where the pets can play with other pets in three separate dog parks in over four thousand square feet of space.

"Do you know why dogs are like phones? Because they have collar IDs. That's a funny one. I like that one.

"A lot of times our clients are too busy to bring their dogs over to us, so we have a chauffeur service that will drive to your door and pick up your Distinguished Dog. I forgot to say, we call all of our pet guests Distinguished Dogs. We will be happy to pick your dog up in whatever vehicle you prefer. We have the standard sedans or we will be happy to give your Distinguished Dog a ride in a Ferrari, Lamborghini, Bentley, or Rolls-Royce. It's your choice. It just depends on how much you love your pet. So far,

I've driven the Ferrari and Bentley on pickups. I get to dress up in a tuxedo with a cummerbund and the whole works. It's kind of fun for a change. Mostly what I do is spend time with the Distinguished Dogs. You know, this is more than I've talked to a human in maybe a year."

"You're doing great. Tell me more."

"Well, when I'm with the boys and girls, I get to groom them, you know, their pawdicures, vitamin baths, rejuvenating massages, body wraps. I also get to help them with their daily teeth cleaning. We have stylists who specialize in fine haircuts and blowouts. You really couldn't ask for a better place to work if you love pets. And I get to meet their famous owners. I never talk to them, just nod and smile. But I talk to their pets, and I'm sure they let their owners know how good I am to them."

14

INTERVIEW WITH PATTYSMITH

"O H, YEAH. I GET THAT A LOT. Folks are always asking me what it was like to live with Sam Shepard. Or better yet, they ask me if I'll sing 'Because the Night.' You know, we look so much alike. I'm what … five feet two, one hundred eighty pounds, and Patti with an 'i' is like maybe five feet ten and a bean pole, so the resemblance pretty much ends with the same last names. So I say, 'Sam Shepard the guy who wrote *True West* or Sam Sheppard the guy who killed his wife Marilyn in 1954?' What a difference a letter can make.

"My real name's Patricia, you know, named after Patricia Neal because both my parents loved her so much. They saw every film she ever made and some of them over and over so many times that if you sat on the couch in the living room between them lounging in their papa-bear- and mama-bear-sized easy chairs and watched their lips instead of the TV screen you'd see them both mouthing every word Patricia said. It was kind of touching and scary at the same time. Of course my favorite was *Breakfast at Tiffany's*; probably watched it at least thirty times in my life. Mom liked her best as Alma the housekeeper in *Hud*. Can you just imagine what it would be like to work alongside Paul Newman? Oh, my god. I'd just die and go to heaven right then and there. Dad's favorite was *The Subject of Roses*, you know, the one where she was nominated for the Oscar, but got beat out to a tie by Katharine Hepburn and Barbara Streisand. What a pair. So totally different. One the Funny Girl, the other who didn't even show up to accept the award.

"You know Patricia had five kids with that creepy kids' author, Roald Dahl. I had four kids, too. Well, four that lived, that is. There was Ophelia, Lucy, Theo, and Tessa. There was a fifth, but I don't even like to mention her name. I named my kids after Patricia's kids, same order, same spelling, but mine are Ophelia Smith, Lucy Smith, Theo Smith, and Tessa Smith. I refused to have a fifth, had my tubes tied to prevent it, and made my husband get snipped too so we'd be doubly sure we didn't have another who would die of measles or some other awful disease at age seven. Poor Patricia. How awful that must have been.

"Only my very close friends get to call me Patty. I prefer to be addressed as Patricia, and every time I hear someone call me Patricia or see Patricia written on a piece of mail or on an email, my face literally flushes, because I'm thinking of poor Patricia Neal and how she suffered through so much. That affair with Gary Cooper who was married at the time, which by the way was the reason, no not the reason, but I guess an excuse I used when I decided to have my affair, thinking if the real Patricia could do it then I could do it. But it damn near ruined her life for a while. Warner Brothers fired her and she had that abortion and went back to Broadway for a while. And I guess it damn near ruined my life, but I had no Broadway to go back to, so I just stayed with my husband and gained all this weight — which of course is the only reason I'm not confused with Patti Smith with an 'i.' People would say what was it like to work with Bruce Springsteen and write that amazing song, but I'd ignore them and steer the conversation back to that twisted husband writer of Patricia who wrote those scary stories, some that I would refuse to read to my four children, like *The Witches* or *The Twits*, but there were a couple I liked, like *James and the Giant Peach* and *Charlie and the Chocolate Factory*. What a character that Willy Wonka and especially in the movie played by Gene Wilder. I so loved Gene Wilder, dreamed about having his babies so many times I almost thought about having a fifth child and breaking the Patricia Neal curse by naming it Gene, whether it was a boy or girl. But he already had a wife he loved dearly, that *Saturday Night Live* comedian that died of cancer, but I thought about heading out to Hollywood to look him up a few months after she was gone, but little Tessa got sick and I had to stay home and trade my bus ticket in so I could buy the necessary drugs for her treatment.

"But you know, old Roald stood by my Patricia for a long time after she had her strokes, dedicated himself to helping her rehabilitate, took her to London where he hired the best therapists, but still, he couldn't help himself, had to start diddling Patricia's best friend Liccy, and when Patricia found out, that was it, no more Roald Dahl to kick around, divorced him on the spot. I probably would have divorced Ronald when I found out about his little tart Alicia if I hadn't understood the need to play around a little myself. Yes, his name is Ronald. I knew I'd never find a Roald like Patricia did, but again, it's that one-letter thing, just remove an 'n' and Ronald becomes Roald.

"I spent a lot of time dating a whole series of Ronalds, trying to find the best one for me, the right fit with someone like me, someone who might sing songs with a rock band or spend time with a genius like Sam Shepard, or maybe end up on Broadway someday playing Maggie in *Cat on a Hot Tin Roof*. Most of them were complete and total duds or nut cases, like Ronald Number

Twelve who was a taxidermist in Elko, Nevada, or Ronald Number Thirty-Three who wore the signs on street corners to advertise for jewelers or new coffee shops or low-income housing tracts. But this Ronald, my current Ronald, the one who fathered my four kids, Ronald Smith, he's a writer, so that's kind of close to Patricia's Roald. He's a technical writer with a company that sells toys and games for kids, no scary ones like Roald Dahl's books, but my Ronald gets to write all the user manuals and instruction guides and anything else for the toys and games that have words. Sometimes he even gets to make up the title. This Ronald lets me say his name with kind of a silent or more like a soft 'n,' so it sounds a little less like Ronald and lot more like Roald. This Ronald lets me live out my fantasies, and sometimes, I help him live out his, especially when I get to play the role of Patricia Neal in any of her movies. Is this the kind of stuff you wanted me to talk about, because I can talk about it all day long?"

Before the interviewer could nod or respond affirmatively, trying to close her gawking mouth, bewildered as she was, Patty continued.

"Because if you want me to talk about other topics, I can do that, too. I can tell you about the time I left Ronald for a week, left him with all four of the little ones, oh, I forget exactly what year it was, but I scraped up enough money over a few months by cutting out coupons and saving fifty cents on a box of Fruit Loops here and seventy-five cents on ketchup on special there, until I had nearly a hundred dollars that Ronald knew nothing about, so I made up a story about why I had to take a bus to Boston, something to do with a convention for work, something I never talked to him or much of anybody about, so he didn't ask questions, except about where the diapers were and if any of the kids had allergies to anything, especially chunky peanut butter, because what he did best was spread peanut butter on Kilpatrick's sandwich bread. So, I take my hundred dollars, spend forty dollars on the round-trip bus ticket to Boston and the rest of it for a room so I can spend the night in the same city where Patricia Neal receives her Lifetime Achievement Award.

"I got there almost six hours early so I could see the special screening of *A Face in the Crowd*. Roy Scheider was there too, getting his lifetime award, but I didn't care so much about him, couldn't wait until he got off stage so I could see Patricia Neal live and in person for the first time in my life, something my parents could never say. So if somebody walked up to me on the street or, better yet, showed up to my office on my lunch break, like you did today, and asked me, Who would you rather be? Patti Smith with an 'i' who had a raging affair with Robert Maplethorpe before he became really famous, Patricia Neal whose daughter Olivia died of measles, damn, I wasn't supposed to say her name, never say her name, but it's okay now because I won't have any more kids, but I may have to spend a week or so waking up in cold sweats thinking about poor Olivia being cared for by her sad parents Patricia and Roald, or would you rather be Patty Smith with a 'y,' the one who married Ronald Smith, the one who when she writes his name on applications and tax returns often forgets to include the 'n'?

"You ask me that question and know what you'll get for an answer? I am a little bit of all three, depending on the day, depending on my mood, whether I've watched one of Patricia's old movies or whether I've put on Patti Smith's *Horses* or *Banga,* or whether I've just taken one of my grandchildren trick-or-treating around a high-end neighborhood that gives out whole candy bars to every kid who shows up and rings the doorbell that buzzes them with a little shock when they do. I can play them all just fine, the sad parts, the happy parts, the raunchy parts when I'm imagining being on a yacht with Gary Cooper or in a hay loft on a ranch with Sam Shepard, or with Ronald the tech writer at the local drive-in, trying to relive our youths by fooling around and fogging up the windows."

15

Interview with PoolSmith

"Sorry for being a pain with the microphone. I thought it wouldn't make sense if we were sitting at a table, me speaking into a microphone sitting down, rather than doing what I do, moving around a table, so I think the portable mic will provide you with much more fruitful results with me on the move. Is this working for you? Test? Test?"

"Yes. It's just fine. Because I haven't used the portable before I'll want to adjust it some, so keep talking. Tell me where we are, what we're doing here."

"Where we are is Fast Eddy's pool hall — or billiard parlor, if you will — in Capitola, California. For the sake of this interview with, well I guess I can't use your real name, so I'll just call you Smith, for this interview with Smith, I'll be using the pseudonym PoolSmith. Smith here told me to pick a name appropriate to the study, and appropriate to me, so I chose PoolSmith. Someone who is an expert with guns is a gunsmith, someone who works with iron is a blacksmith, and me, well, I play a little pool, or I should say a lot of pool, so I'm the PoolSmith. I know the owners here, they actually give me a key so I can practice when no one else is around, so we're here a couple of hours before real customers arrive. How's that? Test. Test."

The author gave him a thumbs-up and nodded. "Keep going." She sat at a small wooden table a few feet away from the pool table, and sipped a coffee.

"What you see in front of you is a 1948 Brunswick Anniversary model drop-pocket table, which means no ball returns." He dropped the cue ball in the side pocket and retrieved it to prove it had dropped and not rolled down to the end like cheaper model tables. "I'm going to start by placing all fifteen balls in a line in the middle of the table about three inches apart. And I'll set the cue ball a few inches away from the first ball in the line. This is one of my exercises, part of my two- to three-hour practice routine. I'm going to try to sink all fifteen balls in fifteen bank shots, which means I have to put a little low English on the cue ball when I stroke it, so the ball will pull back and leave me a shot for the next ball in the corner pocket, without upsetting any of the other balls in the lineup. Like so."

He shot the first four balls in the corner pocket as if the balls, his cue, and his arms were automated, never missing.

"I'm a little off on this one, so I need to reverse my English, pull the cue ball back so it bumps the rail lightly and spins off at a reverse angle, leaving me in good shape for the next shot. Shape is what we call the position of the ball after sinking the intended ball. Half the battle is making the intended ball, the other half is leaving yourself shape so you can easily sink the next ball. Well, there's actually a third factor that goes through the minds of, of poolsmiths, as they approach the shot. Making the ball, leaving shape for the next ball, but like in chess, thinking ahead, leaving the cue ball in such position that the shape on the upcoming shot will be perfect as well.

Always thinking at least one ball ahead. But really, I survey the whole table first and draw a little photographic map of where I would like the ball to end up on the felt for every shot. I don't know if you can tell yet, but I absolutely love everything about this game. We have fifteen balls here on this table, plus the cue ball. If you look around the room here, twenty of these tables look the same: four-and-a-half-by-nine-foot tables with fifteen balls and six pockets. The main game that folks who walk in off the street play is eight ball. I don't play that much anymore, as it's not really the players' game anymore. They do still have a few tournaments, and I'll play them occasionally, but it's not my love. What players play on this table—and when I say players, I mean folks that usually show up and match up with an opponent and play a cash game. Lots of variations on the cash games. Maybe I'll tell you more about that later. Anyway, players on this table usually play nine ball. That means we take balls number ten through fifteen off the table."

He scooted around the table and dropped six balls in six different pockets.

"Then we take the rack and form the remaining nine balls into a diamond, the one ball on the white spot, the nine ball in the middle. Objective of the game is to make the nine ball before your opponent."

He racked the balls and moved to the break end of the table.

"You set your cue ball an inch or so away from the imaginary line that runs between the spot and the side rail, pull a few practice strokes, then fire."

He let loose with his cue stick into the cue ball, which cracked into the one ball, the remaining balls smashing into rails, each other, and a couple of them into pockets.

"I made the three ball and five ball. Now I have to shoot the rest in order, beginning with the one ball." Which he sunk, followed by six more balls with only the nine ball remaining.

"Notice how my cue ball is lined up a few inches behind the nine ball, pointed straight at the pocket?" He pushed the cue ball gently into the nine ball, which dropped quietly into the pocket. "That's the goal. Try to sink all the balls without your opponent getting a shot. It doesn't happen all that often, but good players can run ten racks in a row. Some folks play a friendly game for one or two dollars a game, and others will play very high-end games, like a thousand dollars for the first to win ten games. That's a pretty high-stakes game."

The interviewer was reluctant to interrupt him because he was on such a roll, but raised her hand, and he pointed at her as if calling on a student. "Sorry," he said. "They call me Professor around here, partly because I do a lot of research and study and practice, and partly because I'm a teacher, so yes, you may speak." He smiled.

The interviewer asked, "What kind of stakes do you usually play?"

"Oh, I don't gamble anymore. I used to, but it changed everything for me. Blood pressure went up. I would sweat more, and when your fingers get sweaty the cue doesn't flow well through your fingers and messes up your stroke, which messes up your game and costs you a lot of money, especially if you're playing for a thousand dollars a set or more. Which I did, back then. The other thing I didn't like about gambling was the money exchange. Of course I wasn't happy when I lost my own money, even though I never gambled more than I could afford. But what I really didn't like was when I beat someone who really couldn't afford it and shouldn't be betting. There's this whole other psychological aspect to the game which comes into play when you gamble. There's this concept called 'weight,' where if one player is better than the other player, and they usually both know it, the better player gives the weaker player weight, in the form of a handicap based on the number of balls that each has to make.

"So let's say you and I are playing and I know I'm a lot better than you, and we want to gamble, I might say to you, 'I'll give you the seven and the eight ball.' That means I can only win by sinking the nine ball, but you can win by sinking the seven, eight, or nine ball. That's a lot of weight. But if I'm significantly better than you, it won't matter anyway. Another factor with giving weight when you gamble is that some folks are speed players. That means they're hustling, like what you saw Paul Newman do in *The Hustler*, or what Tom Cruise did in *The Color of Money*. They play below their potential in the beginning, slow their speed down, so their opponent thinks that they are fairly even. The intent of speed play is for the better player to jack up the bet after he or she has lost a few smaller bets, then take the opponent to the cleaners by upping the speed. I never liked that kind of play, but you kind of fall into it when you gamble. So I don't gamble anymore.

"I only play in tournaments these days, or I'll teach someone else how to play and they pick up the tab for the table. I'm so much happier when I play, more relaxed, no sweat clogging up my play, and I practice because I want to get better for myself, not to rob someone of their paycheck. Anyway, that's nine ball. Nine ball's okay, but it's a glitzy, flashy, in-a-hurry kind of game that can end with one stroke if the nine ball gets pocketed off another ball. It's not at all my favorite game. Probably number four on my list."

The interviewer smiled and raised her hand, but when he said, "Yes, I'll tell you my top three," she put her hand back around her coffee cup. "On this regulation table I have two favorite games. Straight pool is my third favorite game. You rack up all fifteen balls." He did. "You bring the cue ball back behind the imaginary breaking line, a couple inches to the right of where you break for nine ball, and you play what's called a safe break, intention being to leave your opponent without a shot. You have to put a little inside English on the ball, which kills the spin after it touches the rack and bounces into the back rail, kind of reverses the flow and shoves the ball back into the rack with no leave for your opponent."

He stroked three times and on the fourth spun the cue ball, which struck the first ball in the rack and then the back rail, deadening it, bringing it back a few inches into the rack.

"Like that. This game you play to maybe a hundred fifty points, one point per ball. Now, your next raised hand would probably be 'How do you make a hundred fifty balls with only fifteen on the table?' Once you've made fourteen balls, there is one ball left and the cue ball. With one ball left, you have to rerack the fourteen balls that have been made already, leaving the space in front empty. Now the goal is to sink the loose fifteenth ball in a pocket while also smashing the cue ball into the rack of balls to split them up around the table and leave yourself good shots. Oh, by the way, no slop shots in this game, you have to call the ball and pocket in advance of every shot.

"Okay. My second most favorite game to play is also on this table, and is my favorite game on the regulation table. Same initial rack as straight pool."

He reracked the balls, brought the cue ball back behind the break line, and did a similar safe break.

"This time there's one major difference. Well, a couple. The first difference is that each player has one designated pocket that is theirs, one of the two corner pockets at the foot of the table behind the rack of balls. One player has to make all balls in the left pocket, the other player has to make all balls in the right pocket. In an even up game without weight, the first person to make eight balls — any eight balls — in his or her pocket, wins the game. I absolutely love this game. So much strategy, so much use of English and soft shots. It's a lot like chess. That reminds me, ask me later to tell you about the triathlons I used to play with Kentucky Bill Myers back in the days when I was still gambling. Anyway, one-pocket is all about finesse, hiding the ball so your opponent has no shots, leaving the cue ball at the other end of the table to invite your opponent to try for low-percentage shots, thus leaving you a good shot. I've played this game with friends for eight hours in a row. Which might explain why I've had two wives and am currently on a sabbatical."

He walked over to the table and took a sip of water.

A hand shot up while the interviewer had the opportunity. "Tell me about your fancy cue stick."

"Ah. I have quite a collection. This one's Bonny, named after my first wife. It's a Balabushka, very rare, not made anymore. Inlaid mother of pearl, birdseye maple shafts with inlaid ebony, and wenge. Come on. We need to move over to the back corner, where I'll show you my favorite game."

He picked up two cases and his drink and carried them with the pool stick to a larger table in the dark corner. He reached up to the light above the table and pulled a chain, light coming on above the table. The interviewer moved her coffee and recorder to another small table in the corner.

"Now this is a real game."

"There aren't any pockets. This is too weird."

"Not weird at all. Have you heard the game of pool often referred to as pocket billiards?"

The interviewer nodded.

"The real game of billiards, played on this larger five-foot-by-ten-foot table, has no pockets, and only three balls."

He opened a small wooden box and plucked out two white balls and one red ball.

"These balls are a little bigger than the pool balls used in pocket billiards. This one is completely white." He spun it around in front of her eyes. "This one has a small red dot on it." He pointed it out to her. "And this one is simply red. We begin by placing the red ball on the dot at the far end of the table, centered between the two side rails, my opponent's ball on this dot in the middle of the breaking end of the table, and my ball on this dot. There are a few ways to play this game, but my favorite is called three-cushion billiards. Like straight pool, you're hoping to score single points, one at a time. The way you score a point is to hit your cue ball into both other balls — the red one and your opponent's cue ball — but the trick is that you have to have your cue ball hit three rails in addition to the other two balls."

"What?" The interviewer was fascinated and completely amazed that anyone could ever score any points.

"Like this. Three practice strokes, then push through the ball with a little high right English so the ball will hit the red ball on the left side, spin bounce into the left rail, spin into the bottom rail, then the right side rail, and here it comes slowly touching into the opponent's cue ball."

Which it did.

"While all pool games deal to some degree with geometry and physics, and nerves, three-cushion billiards is all about geometry and physics, knowing the symmetry of how the ball moves around the table in predetermined angles, adjusted by the physics of how and where the cue touches the cue ball and changes the intended flow, and nerves. I would give up chocolate, coffee, sex, and fine wine if I could just play this game all day long."

16

INTERVIEW WITH SIXTEENSMITH

"MY LIFE IS BORING. Not sure why you want to talk to me. And I think it's crazy you want me to pick my own name. I won't do it. You do it."

"Okay. You're my sixteenth interview, so I'll call you SixteenSmith."

Smith crossed her arms and leaned back in her chair, rocking on the back two legs.

"And what's with this Smith thing? Don't have a clue what you're trying to do here. I know my boss told you I'd be good to talk to, said I could take the day off and he'd pay me to talk to you. But I don't get it. You got something going on with him? You canoodling him on the side? He's got a wife, you know. But she's kind of a bitch, so I'd understand it if he needed something extra. But why'd he pick you? Coulda picked me. And if you ask me, you look a little too prissy to me for him. He smells like fish. Even after he washes up end of the day. Me too. That's why we'd be a better match than the two of you. Don't you notice the fish smell?"

The author didn't like answering questions from subjects, but this one had taken things so far off course so quickly she felt the need to respond. "I've never met your boss. He was referred to me by a friend, so I've never been close enough to him to smell him. How long have you worked for him?" She hoped this would even out the interview.

"How long I've known Paolo, shit, sorry, not supposed to give real names, I know. Anyway, what me and him do in our spare time is no business of yours or that hag of a wife of his. Let's just say I've been cleaning calamari and such on that wharf ever since I was in my teens, still in high school. You do the math. Made me enough money back then to buy myself a clunker so I didn't have to rely on nobody else to get me to work or school. A blue Dodge Dart that had dinged-up fenders and bumpers, but a good engine, got me where I needed to go without troubles. My kid's still got it, out in the shed behind the old tractor. Says he wants to fix it up someday. Make it a classic. Says one of those reality TV shows will pay him twenty thousand dollars for it. I tell him that's fine with me. Cost me five hundred dollars, so I'd be happy to make a little money on the side, help pay the rent for a few months so we don't have to take on so many part-time boarders out in the old barn.

"So what do you want to know, anyway? Want to know about what I do for Paolo … shit, I mean Paul. Let's just call the son of a bitch Paul. What I do with Paul is my own business, you hear me? But if you mean what do I do from six in the morning until the end of the day, if you mean how do I get to smelling so much like dead fish, well that's something else. I can tell you about that shit if Paul … Paul is going to pay me to sit here and talk to you, and buy me lunch on top of it. That was the deal, right? I get lunch out of this thing too, right?"

The interviewer nodded and waved for the waitress.

"Good. I talk better with food in my gut. And you can bet I'm not ordering fish, and I'm so tired of all those wharf restaurants by now, thirty-five years' worth of eating that greasy crap. Ah, there you go. Gave that one away. Thirty-five years, that's how long I been doing this thing with … him, with Paul." The waitress appeared with an order pad and pen ready. "Double cheeseburger, the works, fries with the chili on top, onion rings. Budweiser."

"Caesar salad and iced tea, please," the interviewer added.

"Figured you'd be a salad kind of gal. Bet you don't even eat meat. Bet you're one of those vegan things. Right? What the hell is a vegan, anyway? Is that like a witch that only eats vegetables? That's crazy shit. Good thing about this job is we all toss back a couple of beers for lunch. Helps us think better. Relaxes us so we don't shoot our mouths off at some of those idiot customers who come out asking for salmon when it clearly isn't salmon season and we haven't had any for months. A couple of Buds makes that shit all better, just smile at those jerks and say, 'Sorry, all out today.' And we laugh as they walk away wondering, 'What the hell?' Paul will drink a six-pack by the end of the day. I'm good with two or three. Don't want to wreck my evening buzz for when I get home, put my feet up in front of the TV, and pour myself a couple of scotch on the rocks."

She lifted her beer and sniffed her hand.

"Still smells like fish. Always smells like fish. Wanta smell?" She reached her hand toward the interviewer, who shook her head. "Yeah. I figured. Too high and mighty. Don't eat no meat or fish, you probably don't even ever smell like fish, do you? Probably always smell like a fresh fucking lemon bubble bath. Well, I smell like fish, I probably clean close to five hundred calamari every day. You ever cleaned one of those suckers? It's kind of an art. Getting it right. That's why I been with Paul for so damn long. 'Cause I'm good at what I do. Nobody better or faster than me.

"Well, here's what you do if you ever want to get your hands dirty and get yourself smelling like fish for your boyfriend. You grab that sucker around its middle with your left hand. That is if you're right-handed. Me, I'm right-handed, so I put a stranglehold on the sucker's middle. With the right hand, you put a vice grip on the head, and tug, not too hard 'cause you don't want to damage the goods, don't want that damn ink sac to spray. Twist it just a little if you need, so the head pulls away from the body. The tentacles and guts will come out with it. Then you take a sharp blade and cut the tentacles off the head, just under the eyeballs. Right smack dab in the middle of those tentacles is a little beak. You gotta squeeze it to break it loose, then toss it in the trash can. Now don't throw those tentacles away, 'cause they're the best part, crunchy and tasty when covered in beer batter. Just set those aside for later. Toss out the head and ink sac. Well, I shouldn't say that so fast. Some folks like to use the ink in their food, so you might need to ask the customer if they happen to be standing there, something like 'You want this ink sac for anything?' Ninety-nine of a hundred gonna make a pucker face like you're fucking crazy and shake their heads, but you never know about that one who might want that crap.

"Anyway, now you pick up the body and right near the top is a chunk of clear cartilage. Rip that out and toss it. If you get one of those squid that has that spotted skin thing, rip it off and toss it. Now you take the tube and run it under cold water, all over, inside and outside, gotta get rid of anything it picked up in the ocean while it was still alive. Sand, leftover bits of stuff you haven't pulled off yet. Then wash the tentacles the same way. That's pretty much it. The art of calamari cleaning. Sometimes they call me the Queen of Calamari Clean.

"When I say 'they,' I don't just mean Paul and the other guys I work with. But them, too. And not just the people who work on the wharf, but them, too. But other folks around town, they call me that, too. Folks I went to high school with started it way back then. Now it's just become a thing. Kind of a nickname. I don't even know if those folks remember my real name, so I guess

Smith is just about perfect. Is this the kind of stuff you want to hear about? Am I earning my free lunch, here?"

The interviewer nodded, took another bite of her salad to keep her mouth full and have an excuse to not answer Smith #16 verbally.

"'Cause I can talk about other stuff if you want. Like the number of times I cut myself with those damn fillet knives. Paul keeps those damn things really sharp. You need to be able to cut through bone and hard skin and scales. So he sharpens them a few times a day. Look at this. Look at these scars. Don't worry. I won't put them up close to your nose so you won't have to worry about the fish smell. Look at these. Must have thirty or more scars. This long one here on the inside of my wrist. That was a tuna. People joke about it, said I was trying to cut my wrist, trying to end my own life 'cause I couldn't stand cleaning any more fish for Paul after all these years. Now that's stupid. I like my life. I got TV shows to watch, and cash to look forward to when my son sells the Dart. And why the hell would I want to end all that for the likes of Paolo?

"Shit I did it again. I don't care. You can cut that stuff out, right? Change it and make it sound like you want it to sound. Except for the part where I told you the expert way to clean calamari. That part you'll want to write down exactly as I've told it. I should probably write a book. Call it *The Calamari Clean Queen* or *Thirty-Five Years Working with Wharf Rats*. That's what they are, these guys I work with. Wharf rats. Scavengers. They grab all the leftover scraps and take them home at end of day, every single one of them. I can't name them all, can I? Too bad 'cause they all have good Italian names.

"Anyway, they all have a large pot sitting on their stoves, and every night they come home from work with the scraps we cleaned off our filleted fish and they drop it in those kettles and have a fish stew brewing at all times. It's kind of like how breadmakers have their sourdough mix going forever so they can keep making their loaves. Same thing. Always some broth in the pot. Some garlic and oregano. Lots of salt and pepper. Add some tomato paste, and any kind of leftovers from the fish. Then you take a loaf of sourdough, heat it up a bit, slab some butter on it, and you dip it in the broth while slurping it down. Best meal ever. I got two of those kettles sitting on my stove at all times. But Paolo always slips me something a little extra. No pun intended. Gives me a few of the nice fillets that didn't sell that day, wraps them up special for me, writes my name on the outside with a little smiley face over the 'i' in my name.

"Oh, so now you know my name has an 'i' in it. Big deal. Lots of names with an 'i' in them. Wait! Smith has an 'i' smack dab in the middle of it. So anyway, Paolo puts the little smiley face, or sometimes a little daisy right over the top of the 'i' instead of a dot. That's why I'm still there after thirty-five years of being the best damn calamari cleaner on the West Coast — if not the whole damn planet. Because I'm appreciated. Because I get extras. So, just a friendly warning. You stay away from him. 'Cause I'm good with a fillet knife. And these scars look good on me, fit me. They wouldn't look so good on you."

17

INTERVIEW WITH GOLDSMITH

"Goldsmith. That's definitely the best pseudonym for you to use with me. I am the GoldSmith. Are we on here? Can you hear me okay? I don't want to get started yet until you're all set up."

The interviewer shot him a thumbs-up.

"Okay. Great. Here we go. Today is November 8. Other than the fact that the United States is nearly eighteen trillion dollars in debt, increasing at a rate of about fifty thousand dollars per second, it's a fantastic week. On Tuesday, we took the Senate and strengthened our hold on the House, so now maybe we can get something done in this country to move us in the right direction and get us out of this Obama-made slump. Right now, this very second, gold is selling at one thousand one hundred sixty-four dollars and twenty cents an ounce; silver at fifteen dollars and seventy cents; platinum at one thousand one hundred ninety-eight dollars and thirty cents; and palladium at seven hundred sixty-seven dollars and eighty cents. I'll give you an update shortly, but I'm betting those rates will be on the rise.

"You know what's not on the rise? Paper money. Do you know what Thomas Jefferson said? I'll bet you know the more popularized quotes like 'Honesty is the first chapter in the book of wisdom' or 'We hold these truths to be self-evident, that all men are created equal.' I know he had a little help with the second one. But that's not what I'm talking about here. This is what Jefferson said that matters to me, to you and me today: 'Paper is poverty … it is only the ghost of money, and not money itself.' Now you may not think that our financial world is dangerous and volatile. You may think that the S&P will rise for another decade. And you may think that the Middle East wars will resolve into peace and prosperity. And you're betting that the Ebola panic will just fade away. I'll bet you also believe that global peace and harmony are just over the horizon. And I'm certain you think that the U.S. gold supposedly being stored at Fort Knox and the New York Fed is still there. Yes, I believe you believe all those things and more.

"You probably believe in the Easter Bunny and Santa Claus and the tooth fairy and that Jimmy Hoffa is alive and well. Not me. What I'm here to tell you is that gold and other precious metals are the only thing that will survive as a place to secure your economic value much longer than any government fiat currency, or debt-based paper investment." He pointed his finger at the interviewer. "Where do you have your money?"

The interviewer had become mesmerized, thinking that the GoldSmith was talking to a larger generic audience rather than her.

"Me? I don't have money."

"Oh, come on. Yes you do. Do you have a bank account?"

"A small one. In a credit union."

"And someday you'll have more, diversify, spread it over a number of banks because you were told banks can insure up to one hundred thousand dollars. But that's total bunk. Do you know what Jefferson said about banks? No, I'm certain you don't. He said, 'I believe that banking institutions are more dangerous to our liberties than standing armies.' Do you understand the implications of that statement, of that fairly serious accusation by one of the most learned men in the history of our nation? A standing army can strip us of our rights, our control of our own destinies, and our right to life, liberty, and the pursuit of happiness. What Jefferson is saying is that banks that rely on paper money, on the 'something for nothing' philosophy, will prove to be, hell, have already proven to be, more destructive to our American values of freedom and prosperity. Do you know what I mean by the 'something for nothing' philosophy? I mean our central banks print new currency and pretend that new dollars, euros, yen, and pounds are available. That means there's more currency in circulation, which means higher prices, which means economic distortions. And at the same time our socialist government creates more 'something for nothing' programs like Medicare, disability, military contractors, war on poverty, banker bail-outs, food stamps, on and on. You know what I mean. Then the government and banks fill your head with this 'everything's okay' propaganda that distorts the truth and disorients the populace. The only way to counteract these lies is to focus on the truths, to understand the truths, and to share the truths with others.

"There are five truths that you absolutely can't disagree with: Number one – You cannot legislate the poor into prosperity by legislating the wealthy out of prosperity; Number two – What one person receives without working for, another person must work for without receiving; Number three – The government cannot give to anybody anything that the government does not first take from somebody else; Number four – You cannot multiply wealth by dividing it; Number five – When half of the people get the idea that they do not have to work because the other half is going to take care of them, and when the other half gets the idea that it does no good to work because somebody else is going to get what they work for, that is the beginning of the end of any nation.

"The government ignores these truths. Governments and banks respond to problems with more spending, by supporting the bond and stock markets, and then we're led to believe that debt and deficit spending can increase forever. But it can't. Look at the crashes we had to the stock market in 1987 and 2000. And then some event like 9-11 comes along and changes the world as we know it forever, housing bubbles are created, and major wars are created. Could it happen again? Could a 9-11-like event radically change our world? Absolutely. I'm sure you could think of half a dozen. I can. How about if a small war turns into a larger war, or even a global war? What if an outbreak of Ebola or other disease, or merely the fear of a pandemic, temporarily paralyzes the global economy?

"And we know that stocks peak and crash every seven years or so. When the inevitable crash occurs, where will your value be? Will your assets be held in 'something for nothing' programs, with paper that means nothing? Let's hear it one more time for Thomas Jefferson, who said, 'The trifling economy of paper, as a cheaper medium, or its convenience for transmission, weighs nothing in opposition to the advantages of the precious metals … it is liable to be abused, has been, is, and forever will be abused, in every country in which it is permitted.'

"So, do you see evidence of that abuse, every single day with nearly every single headline you read in the paper? What kind of interest are you getting on the paper money you hold in banks and credit unions? When you review and consider the difficult economic and political conditions of the past three thousand years, which has been safer, gold and other precious metals, or debt-based paper? There is no question that gold will hold its value and provide you with a more secure economic future than paper connected to a volatile stocks-and-bonds market.

"That's why you can call me the GoldSmith. I can show you how to secure your future, help you build a financial plan to ensure that you and your children and grandchildren will be prepared for retirement, college, that little cabin in the mountains, and the birth of future generations of your family. I pride myself on having my finger on the world economic pulse. With over twenty years' experience in the financial industry, I can guide your economic decisions and help you make the most informed decisions — whether it's for your gold and silver precious-metals IRA, or for a physical home delivery as a hedge against a declining dollar. Whichever you choose, I'm happy to provide you with the most up-to-date market news available. My goal is to help you weather any financial storm, whether the falling dollar or hyperinflation.

"Now is the time for you to consider the proper diversification of gold and silver to complement your portfolio. Now, I can put you into a Gold IRA, which means an Individual Retirement Account that actually stores gold or other approved precious metals instead of paper currency or paper-based assets. It works just like your other IRAs, except it doesn't rely on paper, instead it holds physical bullions or bars. There are four precious metals allowed to be held in IRA accounts: gold, silver, platinum, and palladium. There is an approved bar or coin format required by the IRS. We call these accounts Gold IRAs because gold is by far the metal most stored by our clients. To comply with IRS requirements, all IRAs, including precious-metals IRAs, must be in the possession of a trustee or custodian. Therefore, legally speaking, precious metals in an IRA are in the custody of the trustee or custodian, not the IRA owner. IRS Publication 590 specifies that for all IRAs, 'the trustee or custodian must be a bank, a federally insured credit union, a savings and loan association, or an entity approved by the IRS to act as trustee or custodian.'

"Many trustees/custodians use civilian (private) depositories, which may be approved by various commodities exchanges, for storing IRA metals. Security features may include timed locks and automatic re-locking features, 24/7 monitoring, and motion, sound, and vibration detectors. They typically have large insurance policies, with some amounting to as much as one billion dollars. There are two types of Gold IRA storage permitted in depositories: non-segregated, where your assets are mixed with the assets of others; and segregated, where your assets are held separately from other people's assets.

"So, what do you think? Are you ready to convert your assets to a Gold IRA?"

The interviewer didn't know what to say. While she was truly fascinated by this Smith … this GoldSmith, she had no idea someone would use her interview as an opportunity for a sales pitch. That he had turned this around on her without her saying more than ten words was truly amazing.

She finally spoke. "As I mentioned, I have no assets to convert. I work, and I rely on what you call the 'something for nothing' policies of our government, what I like to call social welfare or taking care of each other. And another thing …"

She reached over and turned off the recorder.

18

INTERVIEW WITH GARCIASMITH

"**I** GOT TO TELL YOU STRAIGHT UP, don't know why you want to talk to me for this thing. Right off, I ain't no Smith. My boyfriend says, he says, 'Don't you go making up no Smith name. You got brown skin and there ain't never been no Smith I know with brown skin.' 'Cept maybe Will Smith; but that brown skin is really black skin. Anyway, he says don't do it. Don't go talk with that chick. But here I am, and you know why? The hundred dollars, that's why. And more than that. I'm guessing you haven't talked to no Latinas yet, so I'm here to represent. To tell you what strong women of color think about things. But I won't be no Smith, or if I gotta be a Smith, 'cause I know what you mean, and all, about keeping anonymous, so let's use the Latino equivalent for Smith, let's call me Garcia — GarciaSmith if you really need, 'cause there's more Garcias in this place than anything else. Both sides of the border. GarciaSmith. That's me. I'll take that one, 'cause it's kind of right anyway.

"I was born on this side, so I am kind of assimilated, as assimilated as a Latina girl can be in this white-owned and -run world. But you notice we are no longer the minority in this city, in this state. Pretty soon we be taking our land back, what was taken away from us by the Spaniards and the whites. Just like you did from the Indians. Not with guns and violence — no need. You think I'm just another gangbanger from the ghetto? You think again. I may live there, but they don't own me. Nobody owns me but me. Papa used to pick in the fields, squatting ten to twelve hours a day, wrecked his back, but now he's a manager, in charge, knows what it's like and he's making it better for our brothers and sisters in the fields. So don't think I got no brains.

"My papa talks to me and my brothers and sisters about how we will change things. Every night at the dinner table each one of us tells the story of the day. What we did during the day that made a difference in not only our lives, but the lives of the people we live and work and play with. How do we empower ourselves and our friends and other Latinos, and even the uneducated whites who think we're all gangbangers. That's why you come to my school and you see me respected by everybody on campus. The whites, the blacks, the Asians, Filipinos, they all voted for me. I'm class president. First Latina president ever at my school. That's what my papa taught us, to find the good ways to make a difference.

"I'm the captain on the volleyball team and soccer team and every grade I ever got from middle school to now, A or A+ only. I don't settle. I work hard. I take the AP classes and I fight with these mostly white teachers, because they need to know the truths they don't know. I mean I like them and everything, and they teach me things I don't know, but I have things to teach them about what it's like to be brown and underprivileged — economically speaking, I mean, not underprivileged in my mind, but in my class, how we're thought of as a people, and I'm telling you now, that's all changing. And I start with my classmates and we make changes on the city council.

"We educate. We don't just throw a dance to party. We throw a dance with a theme. We throw a fiesta and we educate every day, every second, we tell people about what it's like to live on very little money and have to feed our big families and how things can change and how they can help change things. We change the menus in the cafeteria. We get some healthy foods in there, not just the pizza and sodas and candy bars and ice creams, all those carbs causing diabetes, more so in Latinos than others, so it's important to think about what we are doing, what we are eating, who we are talking to and hanging out with.

"We tell each other the best teachers, pass it on, this unwritten networking between us. Ms. Chen we say is the coolest person on the campus because she lets us think and talk and say what we need to say to feel empowered and gives us assignments that make us stretch and pretend we're somebody else and talk about what it would be like to be them and live like them, and she cares about us. Comes to our rallies, supports our causes, when she believes in them, and tells us honestly when she doesn't and why she doesn't and presents rational arguments, teaches us to do the same, so if we don't get put in Chen's classes, we go to the office and ask to be changed, and we make sure we get to think and talk with teachers like her. Mr. Carlson, Mr. Rodriguez, Coach Michelle, and we got the best principal around. And we got the best football team around, and we go to the games and scream and yell and support them, and then they come to our volleyball games and support us, life is mostly good, except where it's not, but we're working on that, putting ourselves in the right places with the right tools.

"I just took my SATs for the third time, each time scores climbing higher, and I'm up over two thousand now and my writing scores are right near the top. Which is good 'cause I'm going to Berkeley next year to study politics and law and play on the volleyball team. Three scholarships lined up so far, so Papa doesn't have to pay for my education, so I can help pay him and Mama back for everything they've done for me. My mama teaches kindergarten, and she starts early educating those kids to respect themselves and eat healthy and appreciate what their parents do for them. So, this is me telling you about me. Is this what you want?"

"Exactly. Thank you," the interviewer said. "What else? What do you do for fun?"

"Every day is fun for me. All of this is fun for me. Sometimes people say I'm angry, but it's not anger. It's dedication and perseverance, and for me it's fun to work for equality and equity and equal pay and making it so everyone is happier and having more fun. This is what makes me happy, and if you think I'm angry when you see me stand up for someone who has a hard time standing up for themselves, well, you're wrong. I'm not angry, I'm emphatic, and I'm proud, and I will keep doing the same thing when I'm in college at Berkeley, and when I get to law school, and when I'm defending other Latinos who have had bad breaks and got hooked up in gangs and whose parents couldn't help them because they were in the same cycles, into drugs and in jail, and when I get elected to public office and can start changing some of the really stupid and disrespectful laws that exist, don't call it anger, 'cause it's not. It's me doing what I know is right and smart for my people and for all people everywhere. This is fun for me, knowing what I want to do, what I have to do, and doing the things I need to do to achieve my goals. Nobody in my family has ever gone to college, and I'm going to Berkeley, and three of my friends are going with me, and we're going to make a difference, we're going to make some changes, and we're gonna have fun while we're doing it.

"And I have my fun in other ways, too. I love to dance, and I love to party, and I love to mess around with my boyfriend, but always smart, always with condoms right here in my backpack just in case, 'cause I would never do anything stupid and mess up my destiny, and we don't fool around too much, maybe once a month, 'cause I don't want to be ruled by sex and forget what's important, so we make dates and have just as much fun going to the park with a bunch of friends and having a big picnic and watching the moon come up over the river, and talking, talking about when we were kids and our parents and brothers and sisters, and what we're going to do at college and what kind of house we'll live in and what kind of jobs we'll have and who'll be the first to have kids, and I'm always like, 'I will be the last one to have kids,' not because I don't want them, but because I have lots of learning to do first and law school to finish and projects to help build and marches to help organize, so my kids will understand why I waited until I was in my thirties to have them, and my husband will be doing the same thing as me so we will want to have them at the same time.

"You know what else I love? I absolutely love our Cinco de Mayo festivals where the mariachi bands come to play, because my papa plays the mandolin, and he is so good, and he is always smiling this big smile when he plays because he loves it so much and I love watching his fingers pluck the strings and his shoulders bob up and down. That is fun for me because I'm proud of my papa, proud of my family, proud of my Latino traditions.

"There's another thing I love so I guess I would call it fun, and that's when I go to bed with a book and read until I fall asleep or sometimes all night long if I get hooked in a good one, like I just finished Gabriel Garcia Marquez's *One Hundred Years of Solitude*, and I wish I could write like him, think like him. And now I'm reading all of Neruda's poetry and it soothes me, calms me down, and sometimes I think that is fun, to slow down, to get away from everybody else who wants and expects things from me, especially myself, and let my brain float away on other people's thoughts and characters, escape from me for just a while, like floating on a rubber inner tube with my eyes closed, drifting, listening to words in my native tongue by authors who are brilliant, Sandra Cisneros and Isabel Allende, people who I aspire to be, so I let myself relax and sometimes I pretend to be them. Sometimes when I'm alone and have the time, that's fun for me."

19

Interview with LadySmith

"THE MIC IS NOW ON, THE LEVELS ADJUSTED. This is an oral interview of myself, call me the OriginalSmith, or FirstSmith, or maybe the AlphaSmith. I'll decide later on what best fits for this project once I've completed my series of thirty interviews. My primary purpose for this initial interview was twofold. First, to provide a sample of my work as a requirement for the application to the Social Documentation MA program at the University of California, Santa Cruz. The second was to provide, as a supplemental attachment to the application, the required project description of my work, which I'll supply orally here, given that this is my primary method of documentation, preferring to allow my subjects a level of ease that is not always available when also including video documentation.

"My topic of interest is the expression of words by subjects without the added interruption of visual stimulation, thus the audio medium rather than video plus audio, or video plus music. I'm not interested in the artistic combination of sound with image, or the pairing of video with background music for mood. The only interpretation I expect my listener, or reader, to make should come from the words transmitted by subjects, occasionally led by my questions or comments as needed, though I prefer to be as invisible as possible as the interviewer. I guess I prefer to be thought of more as the recorder during the actual process of recording than an active participant in a conversation. My intent is not to record a dialogue but ideally a monologue that the subject is directing at me, or at my recorder.

"My working title for this project is *Smith: An Unauthorized Fictography*. I don't know if the title will stick by the time I complete the interviews and have listened to the stories of thirty subjects, but for now, it's my guiding principle — one that helps me identify and interview specific subjects. By explaining my choice of a working title, I may shed a little light on my goals and intended outcome.

"Let me begin with a dissection of the word 'fictography' and purpose of its use. It's not a word I've heard used before, so I like to think I've coined it but I'm sure that's not the case and will eventually do the required research to discover the truth. For now, I'm less interested with the truth and more with what the word evokes, which is how can we ever really know what percentage of written or spoken words are true or fictionalized? Are the subjects in this study speaking truths when they allow their voices to be recorded by a stranger? Do they believe that what they are saying is true, and if so, have those truths morphed into fictions over time, by changing a word or phrase, by intentional or accidental embellishment? Do the subjects care more about their recorded impressions, even though they are captured anonymously, playing to the audience, so to speak, making themselves, their lives, sound and look better or more interesting than they really are?

"I can't predict or assign a degree of truth to what is said by subjects. All I can do is describe what they've provided me in verbal recordings, a combination of intentional or unintentional fictions combined with personal autobiographies and perceived biographies of others. If the long list of authors, including James Frey, author of *A Million Little Pieces*, or Misha Defonseca, who wrote *Misha: A Mémoire of the Holocaust Years*, or Forrest Carter of *The Education of Little Tree*, had simply included the word 'fictography' in their titles — or at least in their subtitles or first paragraphs of the jacket-cover language — life would not have been so difficult for them as they were accused of lying to their readership, of attempting to pull a fast one by tugging inappropriately at heartstrings, and enraging the likes of Oprah Winfrey, of people who wanted to believe the reported malaise of the human condition as ever present and true through embellished or fictionalized stories.

"Therefore, the use of the word 'fictography' in my title is in some ways a disclaimer, a protection device, saving me and my subjects from any external criticism that what they have allowed me to record is in some way erroneous, untrue, a lie, or any other euphemism that might be applied by journalists, critics, or the general public, because in fact, it is my belief that every spoken or written story, labeled memoir or novel or any of a dozen other synonyms, is modified, embellished, improvised, fictionalized, for the sake of telling a good story which lies deep within each of us, in all cases learned, passed on to us by our immediate relatives and long-dead ancestors, but is also equally an innate trait of human beings, an archetypal truth that has been embedded in our DNA since the first breath on the planet. All hail to the universal fictographies.

"Now we come to the word 'unauthorized.' Notice I'm working backward through my title-in-progress. That's because I'm saving 'Smith' for last, maybe stalling so I can really figure out what I mean by 'Smith.' For me, to call something 'unauthorized' is a bit of a ploy to heighten interest in the content. 'Wow!' says the reader. 'If this story is unauthorized, then somebody must not be happy about it, so it must be juicy.' To be honest, that notion did cross my mind as I created the title. I do want folks to read my work, and to use a grabber word in the title is a good marketing technique I'm not embarrassed to employ.

"But when you think about it, combining 'unauthorized' with 'fictography' pretty much balances and negates any question of accuracy, because every single word of every sentence in every interview may have been fictionalized by the interviewees, so what would 'authorize' even mean given such possibilities? Or better yet, every single interviewee may have been fictionalized by me, and maybe none of their thoughts were original, amateur actors hired by me to read scripts I had written myself. Bottom line, I am my own authority and I authorized myself to create a title and a project that best fit my interests and needs with subjects, real or unreal, that helped me reach my desired outcome. In that sense, 'unauthorized' simply means that no one other than me can be blamed for what appears in this project.

"That brings us to 'Smith.' If you look on Wikipedia — as well as other more accurate sources — you'll discover that Smith is the most prevalent surname in the United States, Australia, and the United Kingdom, and second in Canada. In the 2000 U.S. Census, nearly 2.5 million Americans had the surname Smith. I thought of Jones, as in living up to them, or Doe, as in John or Jane. Like Dick and Jane in older children's books, Smith represents for me a common thread in American culture, values, thoughts, and philosophies. It's a vein that touches, taps into, and weaves itself over every city, person, and activity across the country. Smith represents for me the traditional everyman.

"None of my selected subjects are truly Smiths. Even if I had come across a true Smith I wanted to interview, I would have eliminated them as possibilities because their anonymity would have been somewhat compromised. I allow my subjects to take on their own Smith identities if they wish, or, if they don't, I assign them a Smith name. Those that choose their own pseudonyms like to play with it a bit, which brings out more of their unique personalities, which is one of my goals of the study. What are the archetypal traits of the Smith family — of the everyman or everywoman? Patty Smith is a perfect example. I love how she connected her name to Patti Smith the singer, lover of Sam Shepard and others. The playfulness with which she approached the interview and life in general.

"While many of the words I'm speaking here were part of my original application to the UCSC Social Documentation MA program, I've modified a bit, embellished, if you will, built this fictography, but the final result of my application is that I was not accepted to the program. I was told my work sample was too vague, that the written description of my work and intentions was unclear, that I didn't seem to know what my goals and objectives were, that my outcomes and planned measurement tools were weak. At the time I was rejected, I was angry: at the department, at the planet, at every Smith I'd ever known or heard of, and at myself for not having written a more coherent story that would have interested the department faculty.

"But I didn't let that stop my interest in the Smith project. Using the written rejection from the department, I slowly began modifying the language of my project, making it clearer to some degree to potential readers, even if I wasn't certain yet of my goals and outcomes. I joined the Foundation Center, which gave me access to all private foundations and funders in the United States, and I began looking for foundations whose goals and interests were similar to mine. While I never had any training in writing grant proposals, it wasn't much different than the Social Documentation application process, so I read books and articles and downloaded copies of successful grants and taught myself how to say and write what they wanted to hear. Yes, more fictographies.

"I wrote and sent over two dozen query letters and proposals to large corporate foundations and small family foundations and foundations with very specific, unique goals that I had to squeeze my words to fit. And finally, after six months of rejections and thank-yous and 'This is not a good fit with us right now' and 'We only fund programs on hunger,' one small foundation who provides ten twenty-thousand-dollar grants per year for one-year projects got back to me with 'Congratulations! Your study has been chosen as one of our ten focus projects this year in our Eclectic Category, which means you didn't fit any of our primary programs with specific goals and outcomes, but fall into a category that is more experimental and innovative in nature. This is a new category for us this year and we look forward to your final report and subsequent results. We look forward to meeting you and supporting your work with the "Smiths." '

"That's how I got where I am today, sitting in front of this mic, participating as one of my own subjects.

"As I read through my interviews so far, I am concerned about my presence in them. From this point forward, I will try to eliminate myself from interviews, provide subjects with a half-page flyer that explains my purpose and technique.

"Call me LadySmith, as in Ladysmith Black Mambazo, whose music I love."

20

INTERVIEW WITH TALKSMITH

"N O QUESTION. IT'S TALKSMITH FOR ME, because that's what I do best. That and volunteer. I volunteer for anything and everything. My sweetie's a poet and a scientist, was a scientist, still is a poet, but retired from his life as a physics genius a few years ago, so now he sits in front of the computer all day long working on his poetry and emails and newsletters. He is a wonderful, sweet man and I love him very much, but I'm only seventy-one years old, and I have twenty or thirty years left in me, so I need to keep busy, need to feel like my work is just as important as his work, so I volunteer.

"As you can probably tell from my accent, I am from Germany, so I tutor students who come here from Germany, help them learn to speak English a little better so they feel more comfortable with their new lives here. Do you know about the Hitler Youth that they sent away to the army when they were only

125

thirteen years old? It was criminal. Criminal what they did to those poor young things who barely had time to grow in their pubic hair.

"But where I go every single day of the year, except when we're out of town for poetry readings, is to the Grey Bears facility over on Chanticleer, where I work with all those people who need help every single day of their lives. You know it's terrible to get old and have to suffer through losing your mind, not being able to remember anything about who you are and who your family is and who your friends are. So every single day of their lives, if they don't remember me from the day before, I make sure they make a new friend today by spreading my big arms wide and saying I'm the hug machine. Come on over here and give me a big hug and you will certainly feel better because I know I will feel better. So every day I'm helping them find some clothes that fit or picking out a book for them and sometimes I even read to them, to help keep their minds sharp and my mind sharp.

"And even though it's not volunteering, I like to work every day in my garden. See my hands. They're always dirty but when I see the dirt under my fingernails it reminds me how alive I am, how I love to dig in the dirt and make things grow right in my own backyard, help things grow strong, just like the people at Grey Bears, and you know, not all the grey bears are grey, some of them still have a little brown or black hair scattered around their temples, or mostly they have no hair at all, so it's not quite right to call them grey bears when they are bald. The men, that is; not the women. The women don't go bald. And I'm not sure why that is. It must have something to do with having babies and having estrogen in their systems.

"It's so crazy what women's bodies have to go through. It's not really fair that men can't have the babies and suffer through menopause like we do, because they can't really know us fully if they can't relate to what our bodies and minds are going through as our bodies and body parts shrivel. Even if they are sweet and supportive like my sweet poet is, even when they bring you cold washrags for your forehead and fix you chicken soup with barley and mushrooms and a few green onions and a dozen or so cloves of garlic, and spoon-feed you when you're too tired and sick to lift your own hand to drop a few ccs of broth down your own throat. Even then they can only understand just a little, because they aren't plugged into your bloodstream and psyche.

"Which is why I like to work with the older women grey bears down at the center, because we have commonalities, things that we share as women that no man can share with us. I'll comb their hair and if they've kept it long, I'll do a little French braid for them, and if they haven't kept it long I tell them they should, tell them to let it grow longer for a few months because they deserve to have a beautiful braid draped down their back, a beautiful grey braid, and I tell them I will always be there to braid it for them if they'll only grow it long, and they smile and nod their heads and say, 'Yes that's a very good idea,' and the next time I see them their hair will be trimmed and short and they have forgotten everything I told them.

"Which is why it is so sad to work with old people and so sad to get old, and which is why I started pinning notes on them that say, 'Don't cut your hair, because' … hmm … 'because TalkSmith will braid your hair for you when it gets long enough.' But somebody probably takes the notes off them and throws them away because they always come back with hair too short to braid, so I do other things for them. Find them new wardrobes from our clothing sections and find them glasses so they can read the books I pick out for them, like this one sweet old woman with hair too short to braid who I told needed a good book to read at night before she went to sleep so she could get a good night's rest, because a good night's rest is the start to a wonderful new day.

"Like me, every night I make sure I'm in bed by ten with a good book in my hand to help put me to sleep by ten thirty, and I wake up at six thirty every morning, getting my full eight hours' sleep in before I get on my feet and do my morning yoga, which I do every day, so I take her by the elbow over to the bookshelf with me and I grab a book of poetry off the bookshelf that just happens to be written by my sweetie because we have too many copies in our garage, so I brought ten of them down here to Grey Bears to give away to those folks who need a good night's sleep, so I pull it off the shelf, and show her the autograph by my sweetie, and I read the first poem on the first page to her so she'll see how good it is and how it will help her get a good night's rest, the one about nuclear fusion and how it compares with the beginning of life when the sperm meets the egg, and she smiles and I know she will love this book and thank me next time she comes in, that is if she remembers me next time, but if she doesn't, I'll give her a big hug and she'll have another new friend for another new day.

"I also help sign up the new people, help them fill out the forms to become a member so they can get food delivered to their houses for free on Friday mornings, a big bag full of loaves of bread and fresh vegetables and other healthy things to help their bodies and their brains function well. Just today, I was helping a woman in her mid-sixties, okay, sixty-three to be exact. We filled out the forms and talked about the kinds of food she could and couldn't eat and I asked her about her mother because I was telling her about my mother who is still alive back in Germany, and she said her mother, who was also still alive, just eighty, had her when she was only seventeen years old, and that she visits her in a memory-care facility every other day and that every time she goes she doesn't know if her mother will remember me — no, not me, her — if her mother will remember her, because of the Alzheimer's, and she tells me that every time she visits her mother she says to her, 'Will you go to church with me on Sunday?' which is kind of crazy, the woman tells me, because her mother is mostly confined to her bed and doesn't go to church anymore, but she still thinks she's going to church and knows her sixty-three-year-old daughter is not going with her, and when we finish filling out her forms, I ask the woman why she doesn't just take her mom to church someday, go ahead and do it and make her happy, what can it hurt anyway?

"And the woman says to me, 'I just don't think I can do that, wouldn't feel right to me, can't believe in a god who would do the things he has done, or let happened, and when I say "he" I mean "he," because no she god would have ever let the things happen that have happened, so, no, I can't be taking my mom to church, not only because it goes against every grain of decency I have left in my body, but because she's confined to her bed.' And I say, 'Well, you can bring church to her, bring a picture of Jesus and some candles and whatever else she needs, and you can pretend to be attending church with your mother. Why do you think she wants you to go to church with her anyway?' And she says to me, 'Oh, I know exactly why she wants me to go to church with her. She knows she's dying and won't be around very much longer and when she goes to heaven she wants to know that I will be joining her there sometime in the future.'

"That's when I gave up trying to talk the woman into going to church with her mom, because it was never going to happen. Just like trying to talk Hitler into stopping sending those poor thirteen-year-old boys off to war. The other thing that's good for me about working at Grey Bears is my biceps. Look at these. Hard as rocks. Helps me give good hugs. All day long I'm tossing big bags of recycled stuff into the big cans, tossing them up and into the can, making my muscles burn and keeping me young and healthy and strong.

"And I help with the compost bins, take the food scraps from our brown-bag and lunch programs and mix it up with rich dirt and make real good compost that we sell for people to use in their gardens to grow their own vegetables, and I take some home every week for my garden, and I'll even go to people's houses and help them with their gardens. And we can give you worms from our worm composting bin to take home and help make your garden healthier. If you use our worms you can help prevent global warming — well not prevent, but at least help it to slow down, do your little part to help save the planet because the planet needs help saving. Because if you let the garbage trucks haul your waste away to one of those awful landfills, when your food scraps hit that landfill it's an anaerobic environment, and it emits methane gas, which is twenty-one times more potent than carbon dioxide.

"So come get some of our worms and I will teach you how to compost. And I'll give you one of my sweetie's books and point out some of the better poems that aren't so much about physics and science and more about why things are the way they are and what we can do about them while we're still here. Do you want to hear about the thrift store where we have the furniture and games and jewelry and all kinds of good things old people like, young people, too, or I can tell you about the computer-electronics thrift store?"

21

INTERVIEW WITH BIRDSMITH

"I'M A CPA BY TRADE, but that's just about money, sustainability, provides funding for the other things I like to do. Let me provide you with a little context first, so you can paint the generic picture of my life in your mind. I'm forty-three. I was born in Santa Cruz at Dominican Hospital, at eight thirty-two pm on June 21, 1971. I have a wife and the typical two kids: one at Aptos Middle School, the other at Aptos Junior High. My wife is an aerobics instructor at a local spa. We live in a nice house off Soquel Drive near Cabrillo College. We were married in the Greek Orthodox church in downtown Santa Cruz across from the library, because my wife is Greek. It didn't matter to me so much where we got married, so I let her make all the decisions because it mattered quite a bit to her. She had over a hundred relatives there. I had ten … eleven, if you count Eliza, who sometimes doesn't get counted.

"I come from a family who used to be Methodists but gave it up before I was two, so I'm pretty much nothing, never indoctrinated with any religious beliefs or values or traditions. But I did the Greek thing, for my then-fiancée, because it was important to her, and she was important to me. Kind of Pythagorean. If A equals B and B equals C, then A equals C. Get it? Sorry. It's kind of a math thing, being a CPA and all.

"If tradition is important to her, and she is important to me, then tradition is important to me. At least for a while. At least for a few weeks leading up to the wedding, and a few weeks after, then we could slip into a normal life. Did you know that the groom has to go out and buy the bride shoes and wrap them up with money inside and send them to the bride's house on the day of the wedding? Isn't that wild? Except we were already living together, so my house was her house, and her house was my house. So I took the wrapped gift to my best man the day before and asked him to dress up as a UPS driver and deliver the package to our door the morning of the wedding. He had to drive out to Harvey West Park and ask if he could rent one of their uniforms for a day, and at first they were reluctant, but he's a smooth talker and told them the story, full of embellishment, just like he did at the wedding when he offered a toast, and they gave him the uniform, didn't charge him, wanted him to take pictures to share with them when he brought it back.

"We had three hundred people at our wedding. Her family has so many friends. I think I knew maybe thirty people. Thank god her parents paid for the wedding: fifty thousand big ones. 'You'll only do this once, and I can afford it,' her dad told me, and my then-fiancée managed to spend every penny of it. Ten thousand of that was for our two-week honeymoon to the Greek islands. Which was amazing. So relaxing and gorgeous. I could live there, but my client base would be pretty weak.

"Let me get back to the wedding day. The ceremony begins at the door of the church. It's called the betrothal service. The priest meets us at the door, where he blesses the rings, then puts them on and off our fingers three times. I guess that's supposed to represent that our lives are now entwined. Once inside, we stand together with two candles. She tells me that one candle represents the light of the world and the other Jesus Christ. Now, let me tell you, as far as Jesus Christ goes, I'm an educated man and I know about Christianity and what he symbolizes, but growing up in my house Jesus Christ was what I heard my dad say when he hit himself with a hammer or jabbed his hand with a carving tool. But that's okay. It's what she wants and is what is important to her so … Pythagoras, you know. Then we hold what they call the *stephana* — two crowns linked together with a bunch of ribbon. Then the priest tells us to kiss and I have to switch the crowns with her three times, again, more entwining or merging together of our two souls. And I do this happily, even though the threes are making me think of fairy tales and nursery rhymes my mother read to me as a kid where three was a common theme like the three little pigs. I do it because I want our souls to merge, even if I'm not sure I have a soul, or what to do with it if I had one.

"Because there are three hundred people at our wedding, and because we already live together in a house that's fully equipped with what we need already, these three hundred folks mostly give us cash, which is great, and also artwork, I mean nice artwork, but you only have so much wall space, and taste in art is such a personal thing.

"Then there's the food. Oh, my god. I was way too stuffed, and drunk, to consummate the wedding that night. Which is okay, because we'd already done it before breakfast, just to take the edge off, calm our nerves a little bit before being barraged by three hundred people. There were platters full of roasted lamb, a whole suckling pig, dozens of spinach-and-feta pies. Kegs of beer, cases of wine, an endless supply of hard liquor. They have a Greek festival there at the church and the parking lot behind it every year, and our wedding ceremony and reception looked like another Greek festival. Which it was, because they love to party. And the whole time people are shouting out *I ora i kali*, meaning 'Here is to the good times that are coming,' or *Na zisoun*, 'Have a long life,' or *Opa*, which just means they're affirming what we're doing, joining our lives together, celebrating with them. That morning before the wedding, about the time my best man — or *koumparos*, as the Greeks say — shows up with the shoes, my wife's mother shows up and feeds me honey and almonds. I can't remember why. Tradition. And then because it's the way it's supposed to be, my best man takes me into the bathroom, lathers up my face, and shaves me, which is really strange, because I use an electric razor. Another weird tradition.

"When we put the announcement in the paper, we have to put it in three different papers, not just one. When we get back to the house in the wee hours of the morning, driven by a taxi because we are both drunk as skunks, we walk into our bedroom and they've messed with things. Rose petals and money sprinkled all over the bed, which we don't figure out until morning, when we see it stuck to our thighs and back in the mirror. But I do have to tell you, I love being married to a Greek woman, and all that comes with it. Love that our kids are half Greek, love all the family gatherings and celebrations throughout the year, love the food. Before we went on our honeymoon, I was a pretty avid birder because my mother was an ornithologist, and because we lived in Santa Cruz County, one of the premier birdwatching locales in the country, she would take me on bird walks every weekend. Dad wouldn't come, bad knees and he preferred to spend his spare time in the garage carving wood. But Mom would take me and a friend to Younger Lagoon, Antonelli Pond, West Cliff Drive, Meder Canyon. One time at Meder Canyon we saw a Northern Pygmy Owl, which is very rare. We'd go to Moore Creek Preserve and UCSC, and walk through Pogonip and Sycamore Grove. I started my life list when I was maybe ten years old. I probably had a hundred by the time I went to college, maybe a hundred and fifty when we got engaged. But when we landed in Greece and the Greek islands, after a few days of just laying around our cottage to recuperate, when we started walking around Athens and taking day trips to the countryside, my list nearly doubled.

"After we got over the hangovers, I found a place in Athens called, aptly enough, Birdwatching in Greece, that offered birdwatching tours, and my new wife and I went on eight different tours while we were there. We spent one day in the coastal wetlands near Nafplio, which is in the eastern Peloponnese. In addition to lots of waders and gulls, we got lucky and saw Red Knots and Bar-tailed Godwits. One day we went to Rafina, the Megalo Rema stream, which is east of Athens. We were amazingly fortunate to see the Baillon's Crake, who, when it gets used to you, as long as you stay very still, will hunt for prey right in front of you, like watching close up through a high-powered lens in a documentary, except it's live, right in front of your eyes.

"I am so happy I fell in love with a Greek woman and that her wealthy parents sent us to Athens for our honeymoon. My list is now well over four hundred, and growing. She doesn't always go with me on birding excursions anymore, says I'm a little too OCD about it now, but the record for the Big Year is up to seven hundred and forty-five. If you don't know what that is, there was a movie a few years ago called *The Big Year* starring Jack Black, Owen Wilson, and Steve Martin that you should check out. Starting January 1, there's a race to see who can spot the greatest number of birds in one year. There's some question about whether Sandy Komito's record is seven hundred forty-five or seven hundred forty-seven, but still. Can you imagine spending every day of your life with binoculars and a camera and recording your sightings of utterly brilliant birds for one whole year? True bliss.

"But I'm kind of on my own now. My wife likes to, as she says, balance her life a little more than I do. I still work, still have my client list. I'm not going to ever be a threat to Sandy Komito's record, because I have a wife and children to support, and that always comes first. But when it comes to my time off, you're going to find me out in the marshes and fields and coastlines hunting for the rare sightings that will make my list grow to a respectable number for a guy who still works forty hours a week. You don't see me flying off to Alaska when I get an email alert about a rare bird sighting in Anchorage or Kodiak. I wouldn't do that. I'm not that crazy. I do get the alerts. I do watch the threads, and sometimes I'll fall asleep thinking about being on the plane on my way to find a Red-throated Loon or Sooty Shearwater in the dead of winter, which is unheard of, but it showed up on my alert Thursday, and I thought, I could reschedule four appointments tomorrow and make it to the airport tonight for a red-eye and be there by Saturday morning.

"But of course I thought that was a little crazy, and of course I didn't mention it to my wife, but all night long I had restless leg syndrome, and I imagined I was walking through the Alaskan marshes with my binoculars focused, hunting, ready for a sighting. Instead, I just woke up with sore leg muscles and parched lips. I bought her an Audubon book for our anniversary, and she didn't say anything, just smiled and nodded, though it looked more like a smirk to me. Fine. If she never looks at or reads one page of the book, that's okay with me. I'll do it. I'll look at it for her and tell her about birds she never knew existed. I try to remind her that she once loved birds as much as me, when I bring out the honeymoon pictures and show her the close-ups I got of the Hen Harriers and Sparrow Hawks at Schinias National Park. What a great honeymoon, I remind her, and she ignores me and flips on the remote to some PBS program, not the *American Masters* series program on John James Audubon, because she makes a point of clicking right through that one before I can say anything, preferring to watch one of her beloved, or should I say addicting or OCD-inducing, British mysteries like *DCI Banks* or *Foyle's War.*

"As you can see, I'd rather talk about the birds on my list or the places I have or haven't been to yet on the Central Coast to spend a day with birds, rather than chatting about what it's like to be a CPA or married to a woman who has an extremely large number of Greek relatives who like to eat very rich food at just about any occasion they can label a party — birthdays, christenings, more weddings, Grandmother's Day, Groundhog Day. Oh, and that's another thing. She's probably watched that movie with Bill Murray twenty or thirty times by now, and I don't like it, think it's pretty juvenile, but if it's between watching *Groundhog Day* for the thirty-first time or watching the genius of John James Audubon, guess what wins?

"Anyway, let's use BirdSmith."

22

INTERVIEW WITH CARSMITH

"I SELL CARS. I've been doing this for twenty-nine years. Me and my brother moved here from Puerto Rico in 1975 when I was nineteen, he was eighteen. We came to Florida first and worked in hotels there, cleaning the bathrooms and the carpets and when there were emergencies. You know, like vomit and blood, other things that happened in a big hotel. We were a team. We had to wear the little gold-and-red uniforms with the dangly things on the shoulders, and the little hats. We shared a little place with a bunch of other immigrants from Puerto Rico, mattresses stacked up everywhere. Like little sardines in a can. We did that maybe four years, saved up some money, what we didn't send home to our families, until we had enough to take a bus to California.

"We stopped in Salinas first, but couldn't find no work. So we hitchhiked to Watsonville, and they needed help in the lettuce, and because we were good and fast and they could pay us almost

139

nothing, they kept us in the lettuce as long as we'd stay. And they also owned some artichoke fields over in Castroville, and when the lettuce was done, they took us in a little van to pick artichokes. Me and Rafael made friends with the owner. He trusted us, and after maybe two years he tells us he owns a car dealership in Watsonville and he wants us to come work for him there. Cleaning up old cars they got as trade-ins when they sold new cars. He got me and Rafael a nice apartment in a building he owned close to the dealership, so we were thanking God daily for our good luck.

"We would strip those dirty old cars bare, get rid of the old carpets with all the stains, pull out all the years' worth of stuff crammed up underneath the seats and in the trunks. You know, like candy wrappers and moldy cookies. It was kind of dirty work, but the boss gave us plastic gloves to protect our hands and paid us better than swabbing floors in a hotel or picking vegetables. I liked that job. We met lots of nice people there, folks who came in to buy cars, and that's where Rafael met his wife.

"The boss introduced us to the daughter of one of his friends who he played in a mariachi band with, and Rafael and she hit it off in a hurry, and she was pregnant pretty fast, so they got married at St. Patrick's Church just down the street from the dealership, and I was an uncle in about six months. Then she introduced me to her sister, so now I'm married to my sister-in-law's sister.

"The boss kept finding better jobs for us, kind of feeling responsible now for our families, given he helped us to find our wives. He paid for Rafael and me to go to the Cabrillo College annex downtown to take night classes, got us tutors so we could learn English better. Rafael studied car mechanics, but I always liked math, so I took business classes. It's kind of like he adopted us, like he was our second dad — although we didn't really know our first dad. But the boss was like that. He was a very nice man and he knew important people.

"He had poker games every Friday night and he invited us and always slipped us a little bonus before the games so we wouldn't be losing our own money. After about two years, the boss made Rafael a mechanic, and he started making real good money — enough to support his wife and three kids now. He put me on the lot, trying to sell cars, because he thought I was a smooth talker, knew how to reel in the fish — as he called the customers — said I had the gift of the velvet tongue, and he would sit with me in the office or standing out in the yard on rainy days when there weren't many customers around and teach me the tricks of the trade. It didn't take me too long and I was the second best salesman on the lot.

"I could never make number one and slip past Fredo Alvarez, because he was born here, went to schools and church with everyone here for forty years of his life, so his friends and relatives and old schoolmates would come in and go straight for Fredo. His real name wasn't Fredo. His friends nicknamed him that when that *Godfather* movie came out. Shortened his named from Alfredo to Fredo. But he knew everybody and sold more cars than all the rest of us put together, but that was okay with me. I liked Fredo, and I was making plenty of money on my own to take care of my family, buy my wife flowers on Friday nights that I'd bring home before I headed off to the poker games. Me and Rafael worked for the boss until about three months ago, then he decided to move to Arizona because the weather here made his bones ache. He sold that dealership to some white guy and things changed for me. The new owner wasn't friendly like the boss. He wanted younger salesmen, wanted women as salesmen to work different angles on the male customers.

"So when the boss came back to town for a visit, all tan and healthy looking, he pulled me aside and asked me how I was doing. And when I told him the truth, that it was bad, that even Fredo wasn't happy, he told me he had a friend in Santa Cruz who owned the Nissan dealership. Rafael was okay with the new owners, because the mechanics were in a union and the new owner couldn't mess with them. But the boss took me and Fredo over to Santa Cruz and the owner there was happy to meet us and was looking for salesmen just like us, even though he was a young Caucasian, too. But that's okay.

"It only takes me and Fredo fifteen minutes to drive to Santa Cruz from Watsonville, and we carpool, so we save on gas, and one day his wife makes our lunches and the next day my wife makes the lunches. And if we work the late shifts, there's a great taqueria just down the street that makes authentic burritos and we go there a lot. We were a perfect fit for the new boss at Nissan, because the old boss trained us so well. Taught us the routine. It's almost like a script, but we don't need no paper to do it.

"We practice on the car ride from Riverside Drive to Soquel Drive. We take turns. Fredo will pretend to be some sixty-year-old grey-haired woman walking around the lot in the rain. He says that to me first. He says, 'Jorge, look out the window over there by the Versa Notes in the corner of the lot. See me standing there? I have short grey hair and I'm carrying a purse over my shoulder and I'm looking at the Versa Notes, and imagine that in my purse I have a checkbook with enough in the bank to write a check and pay cash on the spot.' So then I say, 'Okay Fredo, I'm walking out the door, taking my time, stopping to look at other cars on the lot, like I don't really see her or care about her. But I may stay inside the building for fifteen minutes or so to let her stew a little, make her think we are not hard-sell and won't come running to her in a hurry to try to sell her a car on the spot. I'll open up the silver Altima automatic and sit in the front seat, turn on the engine, let her know I'm now out of the building and in the lot, still not caring whether or not I'll sell her a car. I'll walk over to another car and kick the back tires, like I'm caring about and inspecting our inventory, caring more about the cars than I do about selling her a car. I'll wait to see if she comes over to me first, make her seek me out first.'

" 'That's good,' says Fredo. 'Then what?' 'Then,' I tell Fredo, 'if she doesn't come to me, I'll amble over real slow and say, "Good morning." And if it's raining, I'll say, "Sure need an umbrella today." Just something to establish the connection, like the old boss taught us so many years ago. Or if it's sunny I'll say, "What a beautiful day. A beautiful day to test drive a car." Then I'll pull the keys to the little white Versa Note out of my pocket and hand them to her to see if she takes them. If she doesn't, I'll say, "This is a fine little car. Would you like to drive her?" I'll be sure to call it a "her," establish a sense of relationship between her and the car.' Then Fredo says to me, 'Jorge, you're doing this wrong. You don't play her. I play her. Talk to me like I'm her,' and I say, 'Oh, yeah. Sorry. Hello, ma'am. Gorgeous afternoon. Would you like to drive her around the block?' And Fredo will say, as if he's the grey-haired woman, 'I think I would. Do you have this car in blue?'

"So, now we're on script. I've engaged her, got her talking, got her thinking. Not telling me she's just looking — although most of them are. Especially sixty-year-old grey-haired women without a man with them. Most of them are just looking and this is mostly a waste of my time, and it's probably raining out there on the lot today, and I'd rather be inside with my buddies drinking coffee, talking about football games. I continue with the script, answer her question with 'We might have one in the back or across the street, but I'll have to go inside and have the manager look at the computer to make sure. Would you like to come inside and have a cup of coffee?' Most of them resist, but that's in the script too. If she says 'No.'

"So Fredo answers from the hard-sell perspective as the grey-haired lady, says to me as her, 'No, but can you open this so I can sit in it? I've heard they have good head room.' And I'll say to her, I mean Fredo acting as her, 'Why, certainly,' and I'll push the button on the key that opens the lock, and I'll hold the door open for her and say, 'The seat's pushed all the way back. There's a lever in front if you need to adjust it.' Fredo will say, 'Thank you. Oh, yes. It's very roomy.' He'll be saying this in a squeaky high voice like a woman, and he'll be doing it like he's sixty, instead of forty-five or fifty, slow and kind of creaky, like a sixty-year-old grey-haired woman would talk. And I'll say, 'Would you like to take her for a spin?' It's good to use the word 'spin.' It's in the script. Spin sounds better than ride. Kind of zippy. Kind of sporty. This Versa Note is capable of a great spin. Quick. Clean. And Fredo says, in his high squeaky voice, 'Oh, yes please. I'd like that.' And that's when I'd move other cars around if the Versa Note we're gonna drive is blocked in. Then I'll guide her out of the parking lot, say 'Turn left here. We'll take the freeway.' And Fredo will say, 'How do I adjust the mirrors?' And I'll point to the button on the dash and tell him how to adjust it. And he'll get flustered about it, not be able to adjust them while he's driving, and that's all part of the script, written in there as an option that might happen, and I say, 'Oh, that's okay. It's easy once you know how. I'll show you at a stop sign.' Then I tell her to turn right on Morrissey and take the freeway. We skip the freeway and the ride part because it's not really in the script. Not much about the deal in the ride.

"So we pretend we're back at the lot and Fredo starts. 'Do all these Versa Notes come only with crank-handled windows?' And I'll say, 'No. They come with automatic windows. We have a couple across the street.' And Fredo will say, 'What's the best price you can give me on this car? I'm making the rounds today, going to Stevens Creek and Gilroy to check out prices. What's your best out-the-door price today?' And now we're right in the middle of the script, because we expect her to say that. They all say that. Most of them. Just like the old boss taught us.

"This is the time to get her inside the building talking to the manager. He's the closer. Me and Fredo, we just set the hook. But to be honest, we don't set the hook so well with sixty-year-old grey-haired women. They tend to like women salesmen better than us. But we don't have any here. Boss doesn't like women salesmen. I say to Fredo, 'Come on inside and I'll get you a cup of coffee. You take cream and sugar? I'll grab you a cup and talk to the manager about getting you a good deal.' Fredo says, 'I'll just wait outside here by the door. Look at the other models while you get the price.' So I tell her, I mean Fredo, 'I'll be right back,' and I smile and nod. This is where I go get myself a cup of coffee, black, the way it should be, and talk to Fredo and my buddies about football for about fifteen minutes, make her wait, make her look at the higher-priced Altimas in the front row and maybe she'll change her mind and want to spend a little more for a quality car.

"We'll watch her from inside, watch her opening doors and sitting in driver's seats, and looking back at the building wondering where we are. My manager will print out the sheet we take out and show everybody, and after fifteen minutes we'll walk out together, side by side, double-team like, and the manager will walk up and shake her hand. When me and Fredo are role-playing, I'll play the manager now and say, 'Hello, I'm Jaime,' and hold out the printout and point to the top line. 'This is the MSRP. This is the MSRP minus the taxable. This is my invoice price, what I have to pay for the car. I can give you this car for five hundred dollars less than invoice, today, because we're starting our Black Friday special early, and we'd like to sell you this car today.' And Fredo will say, 'What about the one with electric windows?' And the manager will say, 'Let me go take a look,' and he'll walk back inside, leaving me with the grey-haired woman. And I say, 'Do you want to buy this car today? If so we can go inside and my manager can make you a good deal, but we have to go sit down and have a cup of coffee and talk to him and maybe the owner.' And Fredo says, 'I really like this car, but I think you're playing the car salesman game with me, leaving me standing out here all alone for so long. And I don't like that. I don't want to do that.' Fredo says this because it's in the script. It's one of the things we expect them to say.

"We have two whole pages in the script of things people say to us, so we know what to expect. This is the old boss's script, because he heard it all over the years at his dealership down there in Watsonville. Heard every story there ever was. Especially the Gilroy and Stevens Creek stuff, which makes us mad. Then I will say, 'We would like to sell you a car today. What can we do to make that happen?' And Fredo says, 'I want to know the bottom-line out-the-door price on a blue or red or maybe white Versa Note like that one, but with electric windows.' I nod and say, 'Be right back,' and I head back inside and sit with Fredo and the manager and maybe the owner and we talk about how the 49ers almost blew the last game and whether or not Robert Griffin III will take control of the Redskins again after all the fighting this week and whether or not Kaepernick can beat them.

"We've got her thinking out there now. Got her wondering if she should leave or not, but by this time, we're thinking she's a cold fish. She's just playing around with us and probably won't spend her money with us, so we take our time. It's in the script. If she wants to buy the 2014 Versa Note without power windows, which is the car we want to sell first, which is why it's still on the lot, then we are ready to go. But the only cars we have with power windows are the 2015s across the street, and we don't take folks over there unless we have to.

"Finally, I'll go back outside after another fifteen minutes and say, 'Somewhere there's a white one with power windows. I have the keys here. Let me find it.' I'll hold the keys over my head and point it to all corners of the lot, but I won't find anything. Because I know it's across the street and I'm too far away for the beeper to work. But I want her to know that I'm holding the keys to the car she wants. Fredo will say, 'Can I just sit in and drive and see a car that has power windows?' And he'll say it with a frustrated voice, which is all part of the script, and I'll say, 'Let me go find it.' Then I'll walk real slow and head across the street into the heavy Friday traffic on Soquel Drive and go over to the other lot. I'll hold the keys above my head and point around the lot. I know exactly where the car is so when I get close, I point at it, and it beeps. I do it a few times so I know she can hear it from across the street. Then I slowly cross the street again. This takes another fifteen minutes.

"Finally I get back to her and say, 'I found a white one.' Fredo squeaks at me, 'Can we go over there and see it?' I'll say yes, and Fredo says, 'I'm going to drive over. I don't like to cross Soquel Drive in traffic.' And this is in the script, but we don't like it. But Fredo is testing me. We don't like it, because if they're in their car they can drive away. So now we're close to losing this grey-haired lady. I say, 'I'll meet you over there,' and I do. When we get there, she'll look at the sticker price and discover that it's twenty-five hundred dollars higher than the other car she was looking at. Fredo says, 'Are power windows really that much higher?' And I say, 'This is a 2015. And it comes with the Bluetooth package.' And Fredo will squint at me from the driver's seat as our role-play is almost over, because we're turning off the freeway onto Morrissey and are getting close to work. So he squints at me and says, 'This is a 2015. Well, that's like apples and oranges.' I'll act like I don't understand what he means. But I know perfectly. It's on page fifteen of the script. The apples-and-oranges trick. And I say, 'This Bluetooth package is really amazing and lets you use your cell phone.' And Fredo says, 'Can we drive you back across the street and have you give me your best price?' I say, 'Sure.' I say to Fredo, 'Would you come inside for coffee and we'll get my manager to work with you?' Fredo says, 'No, I'll wait out here.'

"This is when the script is almost to the last page. I go inside and we say, 'Definitely a cold fish. Won't land this one. Just let her sit out there for a while.' And we do. Then I go out and say, 'You know, everybody is really busy in there today. They have people to work with. If you come inside someone can help you faster.' And Fredo says, as we pull into the employee parking lot, 'You're kidding me. You can't even tell me a price of one of the cars on your lot?' And I point to the door, inviting her inside. And as we open the door to walk inside the office, Fredo looks over the top of the car and says in his squeakiest sixty-year-old grey-haired old-lady voice, 'Do you want your headstone to read "I was just a car salesman" or "I treated my customers well"?' I crack up on that one. We both do. That's off-script. I never heard that one before. We laugh about that one with the manager and the boss over a cup of black coffee. CarSmith. Me and Fredo are CarSmiths."

23

INTERVIEW WITH MONKEYSMITH

"I'M HERE FOR A FUNERAL. It's a bit overwhelming being here on the mainland again. The whole process of getting off the island was something I hadn't done or worried about in ten years. But Lois died — that's my mom. She had us call her by Lois almost from the day we could understand language, didn't want to be labeled for the rest of her life as Mother, so Lois it was. My sister and I started calling my father Clark when we reached our teens, which was about the time *The New Adventures of Superman* came out, and we thought Mom looked a bit like Teri Hatcher, who played Lois, and if we stretched our imaginations, Dad looked a little like Dean Cain, who played Clark and Superman, mainly because they both had big toothy grins. But Lois drove us a bit crazy. My sister was a year younger than me, so she suffered through it a little longer.

"We watched every show religiously from 1993 to 1997, made jokes throughout each episode about Mom as Lois and Lois as Mom, Dad not even close to being a Superman or matching Dean Cain's physique, but the teeth were always there, and Dad did have those big black horn-rimmed glasses. They never watched the program with us, were always out at some art show or wine tasting or opening of an opera over by the Civic Center. I was seventeen when the last episode aired and, without *Lois and Clark* to help me survive the madness of our household, I began planning my escape. I was a good student and planned on graduating in January. I loved my classes and my studies, but hated being a high school student. The boys were so immature, and the girls way too catty. I started planning in my world-geography class back in September, knowing two things. The first that I would get out of high school in January, and the second that *The New Adventures of Superman* was coming to an end and I would have very little reason to stay in my house, other than my sister, and that I needed to get away from Lois before one of us lost our lives.

"My world-geography class was an AP class, and the teacher, Mr. … well, I guess I have to call him Mr. Smith, was fantastic. He let us call him by his first name, I'll just say Joe, although he was much better than a Joe. But to protect him, and you, he'll be Joe for now. He didn't teach us through little inane pop quizzes, or give us stupid topics for essays, instead he encouraged us to travel the world virtually, to use the internet to learn about the world, to study the people of the world who were not like the ninety-seven percent Caucasians inhabiting our school. He assigned us one paper for the semester, to be on any topic of our choice having to do with life elsewhere, people who didn't live like we did and, as he said, 'sit at home in our three-bedroom homes with the cat and dog and two children watching TV every night, stupid programs like *Lois and Clark* when you should be studying Lewis and Clark.' That one stung a bit, but the season was over now, and I was leaving all my *Lois and Clark*s behind and throwing myself into the report.

"I'd go to the school library and grab the large world atlas and hide in a corner at a small desk only big enough for one and look through every page, studying every location outside the United States, and while I found Alaska and Hawaii intriguing, I imagined Joe chastising me because I hadn't stretched my imagination beyond the political boundaries of the United States, and I did not want to be chastised by Joe, either in real life or in my imagination. He's what kept me going when *Lois and Clark* ended. He's what gave me hope beyond the mundane existence I was living with the real Lois in my life and the made-up Clark.

"I'd show up at the library before school, at lunch, and after school, flipping through pages, getting beyond the U.S. and its protectorates like Puerto Rico and the Marshall Islands. I was interested in the Northern Mariana Islands and American Samoa, but they were still a little too U.S. for me, or at least I suspected for Joe. I finally landed on Bali, checked out every book on Bali I could, used the internet to find out what I could — which in 1997 was still pretty weak, but helped with photos I couldn't get elsewhere. I think it was the photography that won me over. The lush grassy meadows, the amazing blue waters, and the animal life.

"Oh, I forgot to tell you: as soon as I was old enough to get a job, when I turned sixteen, I got a job at our local zoo over off Sloat by the ocean. When I started, I was sweeping up trash and emptying garbage cans, but once they figured out how good I was with the animals, I helped with the feeding and the grooming. So when I saw the pictures of the water buffalo and monkeys and the marine life, I quit searching for other destinations and decided Bali was definitely my topic. I think it was the marine-life photos that capped it. Because Bali's in the Coral Triangle, it has the highest biodiversity of marine species in the world.

"Anyway, it's October 1997 by now, I'm seventeen, *Lois and Clark* is done forever, Lois my mother is getting wackier than ever,

Eve is sulking around the house because *Lois and Clark* is over, so we aren't getting along, and I spend every spare minute studying Bali, putting together this doctorate-like report for Joe Smith, so I'm spending time with him after school in his room, and meeting him for coffee down at Peet's at like six thirty in the morning before school starts, and he's helping me with the report, giving me books he's found, correcting my spelling and grammar. By the time the report is due on Friday, December 5, I have a two-hundred-ninety-five-page report, complete with photographs, descriptions of all the cultural universals like transportation and religion and sports and food and dance and art, graphs of the rainfall and climate patterns, descriptions of the Bali Zoo and the Ubud Monkey Forest, descriptions and photographs of every marine species currently known in Bali.

Well of course a week later, after Joe Smith read all the papers, he gave me an A++ on the project, and because one week later Christmas vacation was beginning, and because it was my last day at this high school that I mostly hated, except for my class with Joe Smith, he asked me if I'd like to celebrate my A++ with him by going to an exhibit on Balinese culture in the Asian Art Museum and a walk through the Japanese Tea Garden in Golden Gate Park the day after school was out, which was Saturday, December 20. And of course I said 'Yes' and because I was still a virgin would never have expected to end up in the backseat of Joe's car parked in the corner of a small lot in the park and of course I wouldn't have thought about bringing a condom in those days because I didn't imagine we'd end up there, but Joe did, must have imagined we'd end up there, because he had two blankets in the backseat, one so I wouldn't have to lay on the cold seat and the other to cover us up, and he had condoms, plural, a three-pack, and I really had no idea at that point in my life if and how he planned on using three condoms with me.

"After I knew. He only used one, and I bled on the blanket on the seat which he tossed in a trash can next to the car as we left. I imagined he couldn't take it home and ask his wife to wash it for him. Did I mention he had a wife? That was the first day of Christmas vacation and he had two weeks off from school and I had the rest of my life off from school — at least that school — so we met eight times over those two weeks and he had to buy more condoms because we used a lot as I got used to it and started finally to like it and enjoy it, because Joe was a good teacher in so many ways. When I wasn't working at the zoo, I was with Joe. Two years now at the zoo and I had a savings account, because I never spent my money, always put it in the bank knowing I wouldn't be able to stand Lois much longer and knowing I'd have to leave Eve behind.

"New Year's Day was the last time I saw Joe, this time in a motel near the zoo where I met him after work, and after we used up a three-pack, he told me his wife was getting anxious, asking him a lot of questions about where he was, and he didn't want to lose her, and he loved us both, but he thought it might be better if we stopped. I was just learning how and just learning to like it, and I was in love with Joe Smith, and here he was dumping me and I was devastated and lonely. He dropped me at the corner by my house and I walked around the back and in through the garage door and slipped into my bedroom so I wouldn't have to talk to anyone or let them see my eyes. I plopped down on my bed and buried my face in the pillow for about an hour.

"When I finally stopped, I grabbed my report with Joe's A++ handwriting on the cover and I started flipping through the pages, looking at the photos, reading my descriptions, imagining I was there. I jumped up, found a dusty suitcase in the bottom of my closet, packed some of my favorite clothes, my report, went to my desk drawer and removed my bank book, retraced my steps through the garage and backyard until I was on the street walking away from Lois and Clark's house.

"It took me a few days to get paperwork together, passport and tickets for the flight, but within a week I had left the U.S. and everything I loved and hated behind. When I landed at the Bali airport, I had no reservations for lodging, but I recognized things from my report, knew how to move around, found my way to an information center and located a great little hut to rent for a week so I could get situated. I took a cab out to the Ubud Monkey Forest and told them about my work at the zoo back in San Francisco, and they put me together with a few of the monkeys and watched how I worked with them. When they asked me how old I was, I lied and said I was eighteen. I didn't know if it mattered, but I thought it might be better if I sounded legal. They hired me right there and I started the next day.

"Seventeen years I've been working with those amazing monkeys. If you want to know the full name of the center, it goes like this: Padangtegal Mandala Wisata Wenara Wana Sacred Monkey Forest Sanctuary. We usually get about ten thousand tourists a month. In addition to the amazing monkeys, we also have the Pura Dalem Agung Padangtegal temple in the middle of the center, which also attracts a lot of visitors. So, I guess if I need a Smith name, let's make it MonkeySmith."

24

INTERVIEW WITH
TEACHSMITH

"I GUESS YOU CAN CALL ME TEACHSMITH. Or maybe Montessori Smith. No. Let's stick with TeachSmith because I may never teach with Montessori again. After what's happened. But let me back up. I absolutely love teaching. It's what I've done my whole life. What I've always wanted to do. I love kids. I love their brains. I love their parents. Well, most of them anyway. And they love me.

"I don't have kids, don't have a husband, just a boyfriend who's busier than me, so I dedicate most of my life to teaching, to learning about teaching, to creating fun activities for kids. I study the brain, what makes us tick. I go to conferences all over the country to study the latest research. I love Howard Gardner, his theories on multiple intelligences. I'm going to two conferences in Santa Barbara in July, the Neuroscience of Reading and the Emotional Social Brain. Back to back. Two weeks' worth. Can't wait. I love this stuff. All of this brain work ties in perfectly with the Montessori method. Kids are so eager for knowledge. We develop them physically, socially, emotionally, and cognitively.

"Well, I used to until I got fired two months ago. Can you believe that? Me getting fired. Never in my wildest dreams. I've worked in public education at progressive schools, but nothing like Montessori. I've worked at one in Aptos, on Maui, and most recently the one in Marin where the administration totally sucks and has no idea who Maria Montessori is or what the key elements of her practice are. It makes me sick to my stomach. For myself. For my kids. For all of us. Administrators are evil people and really don't belong on this planet.

"Do you see how strongly I feel about my work and my kids? Is it becoming clear to you yet that teaching and working with kids is my whole life? They want to pigeonhole us, make us walk through ridiculous procedures that have nothing to do with good teaching or what Maria wanted. If she were still alive, she'd join me here with you, tell you that student choice is key. You give them a range of options, but they make decisions for themselves. It's a discovery model, where they learn key concepts by working directly with materials rather than receiving incessant and boring instruction. Which is what the admins would prefer we do. Stand up in front of students in rows and pontificate. Assholes. And we are highly trained.

"I have taken every Montessori class ever offered. I'm sure I have the equivalent of a PhD in Montessori by now. I probably spend twenty-five percent of my paycheck on books and conferences and materials for my kids. The assholes won't pay for them. But I will. I'll do anything for my kids. I love them so much. It almost killed me when they ripped me out of my classroom, away from my kids. I tend to drink a little too much, but when they walked me out of my room to my car, I went straight to the bar, ordered two margaritas, no salt. Went home and cracked open a bottle of nice wine I'd been saving for a special occasion.

This one wasn't so special, but was devastating, and I drank the whole thing. Woke up on the floor in the morning.

"Drinking isn't really why they fired me. Although it probably didn't help when I had a little too much at our annual fundraiser and ripped into the head administrator for treating my friend with cancer so terribly. They removed her from her classroom, from her kids, her life, told her they were putting a long-term sub in her room until they knew whether or not she'd live. I should have kept my mouth shut, but I didn't. I don't do that. I believe I'm the smartest one in the whole school when it comes to teaching kids and making sure that Maria's methods guide us and are adhered to. But they made me sign the paper that said I wouldn't drink at school functions anymore, and I don't, I haven't, even though they are still obnoxious unfeeling assholes for treating my friend that way.

"But that was last year. This year was my best start ever. I was at the top of my game. My kids were loving everything, creating and learning beyond expectations. Their parents were loving it, were loving them, and me. But something shifted. I couldn't tell you the day or the event or if I said anything specific, because I say lots of things, speak my mind to everyone about what I think and how I think things could be better. Especially when it comes to the gestapo administrator. He doesn't like me. Hates me. Which is okay because I hate him, too. But he's got the power. Male dickhead. He didn't like it when I flexed my muscle, showed him my power. End of last year, he tried to fire me, but parents came to the rescue. Came out in droves to support me. Put him in his place. I probably gloated about that a little too much, probably made him hate me even more, look for other ways to take me down. Because he certainly did that. Now as you've probably guessed, I can be a little mouthy when I state my opinions, but they're all rooted in sensible Montessori practices.

"I thought most of my colleagues loved me. They certainly drank with me after work, never refused an offer to tip one back. But somehow I miscalculated. Something went askew. Here I am having the best teaching year of my life, finishing the Montessori art book I've been working on for six years, getting ready to publish it, and I'm sure every Montessori school in the world will want to use it, because I've been teaching it in workshops to teachers every summer for five years, and they all love it. But then, out of nowhere, they walk into my room after the last student has gone home, tell me to pack my things. Pack my things! Everything in this room is my thing. The tables I purchased, the shelves I built and painted, the models I built. All of it is mine. Was. I couldn't strip it all away from the kids. Left almost everything. It would be devastating enough for them to lose me without getting any sensible explanation why.

"Anyway, they walked me to my car, told me to show up the next day for the exit interview. Exit interview, my ass. This was a lynching party. They tried to get me to sign a document they had already prepared, probably weeks in advance. Said they would pay my salary for the rest of the year, that they'd cover my insurance for eighteen months. But I had to sign this piece-of-crap document that stated I had threatened the administration with death threats. 'What?' I screamed. 'Are you crazy? I don't even kill spiders. I'm the most passive person I know.'

"They pulled out two more documents, depositions taken from two of my colleagues, two of my closest friends, both of whom stated that I told them I might just have to buy a rifle, pop open the window of my classroom, and pick off the administrators one by one as they sat on the deck of their second-story offices. Are you crazy? I will never sign this thing. I never said anything like that. To anyone. Especially to my two friends. Friends. Or so I thought. Worse than being walked to my car by security guards, worse than never seeing my students again, these two supposed friends set me up and lied to the administration, horrendous lies that led to me sitting here now talking to you about my life.

"Only thing I can figure out is that after school one day, after the kids were gone, my friends came to my room to chat about a workshop that was coming up. One of them brought a bottle of wine. I got the opener from the top drawer of my desk and we popped the cork, each of us having a couple glasses full. But I never would have said anything like what they had written about me. I'm sure I called the head admin a dickhead and an asshole a few times, and who knows, I might have said if I had a gun, I might have to use it. But a high-powered rifle and picking them off their deck from my classroom window? Never. Never would have said that. Never would have thought my friends would betray me like they did."

25

INTERVIEW WITH
KIMSMITH

"GIVEN WHAT YOU'VE TOLD ME ABOUT YOUR STUDY, which is not very much at all seeing as how you want me to open up and spill my thoughts, I guess the name I should use, just to keep in line with your notion of Smith being the most popular surname in the United States, the everyman so to speak, would be Kim, which is the most popular surname in Korea. So, call me KimSmith.

And before you even ask, no, I don't work in a nail salon like so many of my Korean brothers and sisters who make their way over here from the homeland thinking the American Dream is awaiting them. I can barely do my own nails. I do go to the salons to have mine done. I have good friends who work there. Did you know that the United States is home to the largest Korean diaspora community in the world? We constitute 1.8 million inhabitants in the U.S., or about 0.6 percent of the population.

"As you know, I live in San Jose, was born there, have lived there every day of my twenty-seven years on this planet. To most people I am clustered in with every other Asian American group. I can't tell you how many times a week someone comes up to me and says, 'Are you Chinese? Are You Filipino? Or Vietnamese?' It is bothersome that folks don't take the time to understand the differences between Asian groups. Just learn a simple question in Korean, that would easily solve the problem. Ask me in my native tongue, and I will answer you in yours.

"I'm looking at the list of preliminary questions you sent to me. It's funny, because like you, I am a researcher, a historian. My work at San Jose State University finds me hunkered down in the library, out on Google, and like you, interviewing fellow Koreans about their lives, what they like to do in their free time, what their favorite foods are. Do you know that the number one food listed by Koreans is Korean tacos? Isn't that crazy? So many of our tastes are influenced by the fusion of our culture with what we have found here in California. We use the traditional Mexican corn tortillas to house our taco fillings, but we stuff them with bulgogi and kimchi. Bulgogi means 'fire meat,' so you can bet when you take a bite your mouth will explode. And the kimchi, well I'm certain you know, consists mainly of salted and fermented vegetables like cabbage and radishes. There are literally hundreds of varieties of kimchi, many of them enhanced by the use of gochugaru, which is a very hot chili powder.

"Enough about food. We have hundreds of Korean restaurants scattered from San Francisco to Santa Cruz, and I've made it a personal quest of mine to dine in every one of them. I have a blog called *Bulgogi Bites* and I post reviews of all the restaurants and food I've encountered. Check it out. Then drive over the hill and spend an evening at one. I guarantee you it will be a worthy experience, and I guarantee that you will want to drink at least one Hite beer to lessen the fire.

"Okay. I have to be honest. I have a hard time not thinking about, talking about, and eating Korean food. Back to the Korean tacos for a second. They have become so popular that the fast-food chain Baja Fresh has added them to their California menus, with plans to expand to hundreds of cities across the country. I mean, you know Judy Joo, right? Host of Food Network's *Korean Food Made Simple,* as well as being an Iron Chef UK? I planned a vacation last year to London specifically to eat at her restaurant Seoul Bird. Seven days I was there, and seven nights I sat at the same table ordering different things every night. Best seven days of my entire life. Did you know that she was the executive chef for the Playboy Club London before she opened her own place? I try not to hold that against her, though I am adamantly opposed to the male-dominated workplace that subjugates women to subservient roles. I try not to hold that against her, because even though she was working for Hugh Hefner's male-dominated empire, she did at least make her way to the top of the food chain as head chef. I guess we can forgive small digressions for the greater good that comes of them.

"Let me see if I can veer away from food. About my studies, I have hundreds of hours of interviews logged with Koreans who were either born here or born there. I have driven to their homes as far away as Seattle and Los Angeles. I have held phone calls with them, using handheld mics resting on the phone's speaker, and now, given the current condition of our pandemic-laden world, I have Zoomed with folks, allowed the Zoom technology to collect video and audio data for me that I can simply edit later. Who knew about the benefits of Zoom before COVID landed here? I guess, as always, we have to take the good with the bad. Most of my interviewees live in New Jersey, New York, Los Angeles. Bergen County, New Jersey, is hugely populated with Koreans.

"Sorry to drift back to this topic again, but usually in the first half hour of all my interviews you will find subjects talking about food, restaurants in their neighborhood, family kimchi recipes, where to get a good Korean beer. But let me plunge forward. Many folks like to talk about the Flatbush boycott in Brooklyn in 1990.

They either lived there, or frequented Korean businesses, or knew friends who owned establishments. When black nationalist Sonny Carson started boycotting all Korean businesses, it was clearly a blatant act of racism and discrimination. They get pretty heated about that one.

"Others like to talk about the 'comfort women' controversy in the borough of Palisades, New York, where two Japanese diplomatic delegations requested to have a small monument removed from a public park. The brass plaque on the monument was dedicated to the memory of what became known as 'comfort women,' many as young as thirteen years old, who were forced into sex slavery by Japanese soldiers during World War II. So much more they like to talk about, like to share their feelings about, because no one outside of family usually listens to them. Events like the East Sea controversy, the sinking of the Sewol ferry in 2014. And of course, the many nail-salon abuse issues that surface every now and then.

"But let me back up to the 'comfort women.' I teach a class in the evenings about this dark period of history, about how the Japanese occupation of Korea lasted from 1910 until the end of World War II. The class is mostly Korean women, a few men who understand their role in making sure nothing like this ever happens again. I center the class around the graphic novel *Grass,* written by Keum Suk Gendry-Kim. The protagonist is a fifteen-year-old girl named Lee Ok-Sun who was abducted by Japanese soldiers during World War II. Gendry-Kim doesn't shy away from difficult images to comprehend and view. We discuss the traumas and savagery perpetrated at the hands of men. We wonder if some of the men were better than others.

"Give me a topic to research and I'm happy. Let me dig into the history of bulgogi and kimchi on a Tuesday, and follow it Wednesday with an excursion into the minds of those who made 'comfort women' available against their will to men at war. Anything Korean is fair game to me, whether in the streets of

Seoul, Los Angeles, San Jose, a restaurant in Palo Alto, or a nail salon in Bergen, New Jersey. Is this what you had in mind? Maybe a little more of what it was like to grow up Korean in the United States, in this little San Jose enclave over off El Camino between Lawrence and San Tomas. Nobody who was not in school ever spoke English. Lots of shops and markets and restaurants were owned and operated by Koreans. I was bilingual, loved my Korean roots, but also loved standing out in class as a smart Korean who knew what she was talking about and understood language better than most of the whites in the room. I can tell you that no one on my street could speak English as well as me, and they all smelled like garlic and kimchi.

"Was I subject to racism? Of course. Anyone who didn't look, talk, and act like the majority of the residents in the state was considered at best an anomaly; at worst, ready to be shipped back on boats to where they came from. We got called everything the white kids thought might be rude toward us. They called us gooks. They called us *'kim-chee,'* with an extra accent on the *chee*. Even the Chinese called us things, like *'gaoli bangzi.'* And the Japanese used *'chon.'* Everybody had some slur they used to insult people who were different from them. I was always careful. Stayed quiet through my early teens so as not to ruffle any edges. Until I took speech and debate in high school. Turned my world around, made me open my mouth and tell it the way it was. That's when I became most proud to be a Korean, to share my ancestry, my roots, my food, my people with the rest of the world. So here I am, telling it to you.

26

Interview with GrannySmith

"Oh, I just don't know about this Smith thing. How did you come up with such a wacky idea? It doesn't make a whole lot of sense to me, but I guess that doesn't matter much. As long as it makes sense to you. And just so you know, I don't need the hundred dollars. You can keep that or donate it to someone else. I have a nice pension, a healthy little nest egg that will last me fine until I'm gone, which could be sooner than later.

"I don't know if you know this, but I'm ninety-six years old, born in 1923. They had a birthday party for me last month. I don't have any friends that are still alive, so it was family, my great-granddaughter and her girlfriend. They brought one of those decadent carrot cakes from the Buttery that I love so much. I had two pieces. And a card. Harriet found it in some card shop in San Francisco where she lives and goes to school, with her friend, Devon. I think Devon is Irish. They live together now. They're a

167

couple and I'm fine with that. Whatever makes people happy, because Lord knows there's enough out there to make you unhappy. Grab it while you can.

"This card Harriet got me is not your typical Happy Birthday card with lots of colors and things popping out at you. No, it's one of those cards that tells you everything that happened in the year you were born. They both signed it, Harriet and Devon, said 'Love, Harriet and Devon,' and I know Harriet loves me, and I love her more than almost anything I can think of, even the Buttery carrot cake, but how can Devon love me so quickly? I've only met her twice, and I wouldn't jump so quickly to tell someone I love them, because I know a little about love and it takes a little time to make it grow right. So even though I love Harriet to death, I'm a little suspect when I open the card and see those signatures there on the back page of this little booklet, but I should tell you that too much sugar can do that to me, can jack me up and make me wonder about things I wouldn't normally be wondering about, and after two pieces of that cake, I'm thinking about a third, but I let it go, flip back to the front of the card and start reading about all the things in January that happened the year I was born. I tell you. Happy Birthday indeed!

"The first thing I read is that on January 1 the Union of Soviet Socialist Republics was established. I never knew that, and wouldn't have cared if I did. Politics didn't matter so much to me in my life. Then there's three different things about the Ku Klux Klan, in January alone, and I'm thinking what a year to be born, all this hatred and racism and what a bad time to be black in this country, which makes me remember my friend Tanya that worked with me down at the Boardwalk at Marini's Candy. We helped make their famous salt-water taffy all day long for two summers. It must have been, let me think, started between sophomore and junior years, so that would have been 1939 and 1940. There was a war going on and our friends from high school were joining the military. Tanya's older brothers both went. Two of my uncles. Lots of people died, but I don't want to talk about that.

"So then I flip that card to February and see that the U.S. signed a friendship treaty with Central American countries in early February and I wonder why we weren't friendly with them in the first place and why is life so hard sometimes. But then I read that ink paste was manufactured by Standard Ink Company for the first time and that's a good thing, for everybody. And the first black pro basketball team called Renaissance was organized, and I drift back to Tanya, whose two brothers played on our championship Santa Cruz High team before they shipped out. They were tall, lean, strong. I especially liked Tyrone. We had chemistry together. That's funny. What I mean is we took a chemistry class with Mr. Byington, third period, not that, you know, we had chemistry, although maybe we did a little. We always laughed together, joked with each other. I guess that's what lab partners do. But back then a white girl wasn't about to date a black boy, but I could definitely be best friends with his sister, which I was, until the day she died, which is another story, and I don't want to talk about it.

"I turn to March and I see that the first dance marathon was held in New York City and Alma Cummings set a record of twenty-seven hours with six different partners, and I go back to Marini's and how Tanya and I would finish up the last batch of taffy on a Friday, stocking up for a busy weekend of tourists coming over the hill from San Jose, how we'd go into the storage room where we had a change of clothes, give ourselves a bit of a sponge bath, then hurry upstairs to the Cocoanut Grove where we would dance all night long, usually with each other.

"When I get to April, I go straight to see what happened on the fifteenth, Tax Day, because that's also the day that Harriet was born, some seventy-six years later, Harriet who I love more than anything on this spinning planet, and I read that insulin becomes available for diabetics on that day. I remember the day that my Harold was first diagnosed and how it shook us both to the core, but we figured it out, learned about the insulin, both of us how to inject him, how to keep him alive for nearly twenty more years, and it doesn't make me sad, just makes me think about things I haven't thought about in ages, so I quickly turn to May and read about the first North American transcontinental flight that goes from New York to San Diego. I know how nervous I get when I fly and how Harold would read to me, hold my hand, calm me down, the few times we flew together, and I can't imagine what it must have been like for those people on board that first flight wondering the whole time if they were going to crash into a corn field or the Great Salt Lake or the runway in San Diego.

"Reading this card is starting to make me feel my ninety-six years, so after I read the one about how the U.S. attorney general says it is legal for women to wear trousers, I decide not to read everything, to just close my eyes and point a finger and pick one per month. Why on earth would the U.S. attorney general get involved in what clothes a woman chooses to wear? Harriet's friend Devon has worn trousers both times I've seen her, and even though I noticed, it doesn't bother me. I'm more of a dress and skirt gal, and I wish Harriet would wear the ones I've made her. I don't care so much anymore. Things change. People change. The Devon I knew from high school had red hair, freckles on her face and arms, was always there at the dances with us on Friday nights, danced with all the boys, and I mean all. Harriet's Devon doesn't dance with boys. She dances with Harriet. June's finger pointing tells me that Brinks unveiled the first armored security vans. I don't know that I care much about that, but I wonder if banks get robbed less.

"When I get to July and read about two-pound hailstones in Russia killing people and cattle, I'm done with this card, but don't say so to either Harriet or Devon, so I hug them both, distract them by asking for a third piece of cake, and set the card under a wrapped gift on the table that looks like it's probably a book. My distraction works and they forget about me not finishing my perusal of the 1923 card.

"They hand me the gift to open, which I do between bites, and find a book called *Square Octagon Circle* by Ellie Ga, an artsy sort of book like Harriet always likes to buy me, even before Devon was part of the picture. I flip through it, but focus on the frosting on the cake. When I finish the last bite, Harriet finds the card, reminds me I haven't gotten to August yet, and she wants to hear more about what happened the year I was born, so I hurry through Warren G. Harding dying in August, Bernie Neis hitting the one thousandth Dodger home run on September 11, which reminds me of the attack on the Towers nearly twenty years ago, watching those buildings melt and tumble to the ground, and the sugar in my stomach causes a rumble and growl. Maybe it'll be death by carrot cake for me, which would be just fine. I'll tell Harriet that's what I want engraved on my headstone, but then I remember that I want to be cremated and have my ashes sprinkled in Hawaii at Harold's and my favorite beach at Napili.

"On to the first unassisted triple play by Ernie Padgett on October 6, Kentaro Suzuki ascending Mount Iizuna on November 14, and finally I'm done with this card when I read that Greek king George II was overthrown by the army on December 17. I can't wait until they leave so I can take this card with all of its memories and use it to light a log in the fireplace. But I don't really want them to leave, because Harriet is all I live for anymore, and now Devon, but I'm still not sure about her, if she has what it takes to make my Harriet happy, like Harold and I tried to make each other happy, like Tanya and I made each other happy. But I'm ready for a nap now.

"Did I tell you about Harriet? How she's going to law school at USF next year? Well, if I didn't, I'm telling you now. Harriet, my great-granddaughter, is going to USF School of Law in August and she bought me a sweatshirt that says so, one of those hoody things that not only keeps my body warm, but my head as well. She took a picture of me wearing it, posted it on Facebook and that Instagram thingy, and all her friends have seen it. Not mine. I don't have any friends left alive. I've been to all their funerals. They weren't all sad. Tanya's was. My sweet Tanya. Have I told you about Tanya, my best friend? She reminds me of Harriet, how Harriet is with Devon. How Tanya was with me. Harriet's my great-granddaughter, you know.

"So, I think it might make sense to call me GrannySmith. Yes, that would be perfect. Because that's what I am. And, if I had to choose a dessert other than the Buttery carrot cake, my next favorite thing on the planet is an apple crisp with brown-sugar praline and Granny Smith apples. Harriet makes it for me now."

27

Interview with WordSmith

"Funny you should ask that question. Since a very young age I have always thought of myself as a wordsmith. So let's just call me that. Mostly because I love the way words are constructed, words like 'gaggy' and 'zyzzyva.' What letters are used to hang them together? Their roots. Who used them first and why? Take a word like 'alabaster.'

"But wait. Before we delve any further into this venture, I do have to tell you that the process you're proposing is not my preferred form of communication. I read your email describing the methodology, your hypothesis statement, and I love the notion of social documentation, the roots behind your Smith ideas, and I really like the idea of the process of fictography you describe.

"What bothers me about the study design is the minimal participation by you, the interviewer. For the majority of my life,

I have considered myself a dialectician, addicted to the art of investigating or discussing the truth of opinions. Given that premise, I love to communicate through a process that involves a discourse between at least two people, often more. The part I like about your process is that we already have different points of view about the process itself, and that addresses a key tenet of my thinking and work. What remains bothersome is the fact that I will proceed in a monologue fashion to talk about me and my thoughts.

"I will agree to continue with one caveat: that you allow me to interview you separately when you finish with mine. My interview of you, I believe, will be the final interview of your study. Yes, I understand your hesitation. I can tell you want to keep yourself removed from this process as much as possible, but I need to see some semblance of the dialectic at work for this to be of value to me. I'm taking your head nod as agreement.

"One more thing. I'd like to read all your completed interviews before I interview you. Yes? Great! Off we go.

"Back to alabaster. I first learned about it as a youth when my grandmother gave me a yellow globe that sat on a frame. I pored through my *Encyclopedia Britannica* at home and when I exhausted that I went to the New York Public Library and spent hours doing research. It's a fine-grain, translucent form of gypsum, carved into things like globes and ornaments and figurines. There is much speculation as to the etymology of alabaster, but in my studies one thing I learned is that it can be dated back to the Egyptian goddess Bast, who used it for her vessels. And Pliny the Elder talks about its origins connecting to a region of Egypt known as Alabastron.

"That's what I do as a wordsmith. I take a word that I somehow find striking and I dig, I study, I build a world and understanding around the word. Even though I used 'alabaster' as an example, it's not a word I have much passion for anymore, not something I want to spend much of my time on as an adult who is constantly seeking truth and understanding of words and concepts, not only to think about them, but to write about them, to bring them to life in a way that no one has ever done before. I will, however, tell you about a concept, a project, I've been mulling over for the past few months, that will give you a better idea of who I am and how I spend my time.

"By the way, I did enjoy your reference to Studs Terkel's book *Working* and his interviews of working-class folks, and I made a clear connection to your use of Smith as a sort of everyman. The topic is 'exile.' If you dig back in time, you'll discover that in Roman law *exsilium* referred to two different flavors of exile, one self-inflicted and the other more highly visible form where someone or some people have been banished or denied reentry to their home or country. I'm interested deeply in both forms.

"I use a software program called Inspiration, and for me, it truly is a mind-mapping environment that allows you to create links and connections to various threads related to your topic of choice. As I wonder about what drove you into your Smith project, you may wonder what thrust me into an excursion about 'exile.' I'll pretend you just asked me a question about it, knowing that you won't, and that half of me will need to provide my own discourse to the other half to complete the conversation.

"It was a quote by Thomas Jefferson that got me started. I don't remember why or where it entered my world, but it did, and I'm thankful. The quote was 'Public employment contributes neither to advantage nor happiness. It is but honorable exile from one's family and affairs.' As you can see, Jefferson expanded his, and my, notion of exile in this quote, one that still deals with one of the two flavors, the self-inflicted, but takes it a bit further with the thought of removing oneself from family and affairs. His quote takes a prominent spot on my Inspiration mind map.

"Here. Take a look:

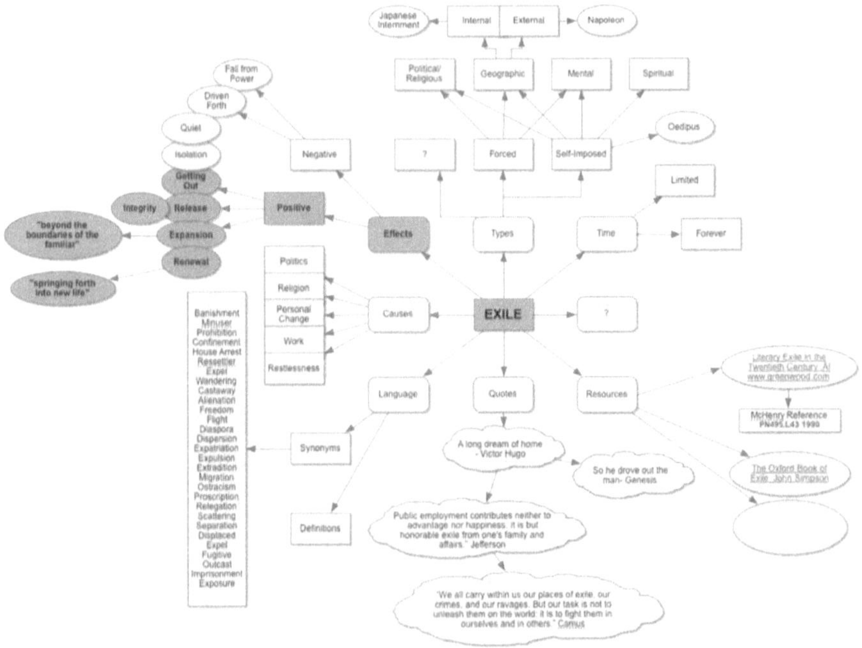

"You'll notice a few other quotes that apply, Victor Hugo's 'A long dream of home' and 'So he drove out the man' from Genesis. You can see that I'm not only interested in cause and effect and types, but given the true etymologist that I am, I have a fairly lengthy list of synonyms. My favorites, and those that I am delving into more deeply at the moment, include 'diaspora,' 'exposure,' 'expatriation,' and 'ostracism.' I also like 'resettler,' because it is one of the few that refer to the self-inflicted brand of exile.

"A friend and I eat at a Chinese restaurant, Little Shanghai, downtown once a week, and for the last month we have been kicking this concept back and forth like a soccer ball too full of air, bouncing off our feet in errant flight, flying off our tongues against walls and neighbors' plates of garlic eggplant, sometimes landing in bowls of wonton soup. No soy sauce added; we like it hot, a bit of doubanjiang or Lao Gan Ma, just enough to keep the sweat of exile dripping from our brows. For the sake of your study, to maintain your required anonymity, we'll call my friend Yin, and to deepen the mystery, I'll slip into third-person narrative and call myself Yang. As a reminder, if we were having my preferred conversation, you would be Yin, I would be Yang, and we'd dive into the roots of fictography, the value of considering Smith as the everyman, the nature of social documentation, and everything else that would naturally spew forth from a never-ending cluster map generated by two active minds seeking truth. Just a reminder. Of what's to come.

"Back to exile, one of Yang's favorite topics. He has been fascinated by the idea since he was a young boy, removing himself from family conversations, refusing to go to temple, pitting himself against others, which always exaggerated and solidified this sense of self-exile. Yin would nod, talk about his own form of self-exile, different than Yang's, different in that it didn't take the form of rebellion, as did Yang's, but rather was influenced by a severe sense of shyness that pulled him into himself, away from others, into his room to read books with flashlights under sheets, to feign illness on days when he was scheduled to present an oral book report, an exile, not completely unlike Yang's, of circumstance and response. Neither Yin nor Yang liked to focus on the all-about-me nature of things, so of course moved the thought of exile outside their personal experiences, Yang offering up the Dalai Lama as an example of self-imposed exile, a survivor's approach to Chinese anti-religious legislation. Yin wasn't sure if the Dalai Lama would agree that it was self-imposed, that the exile was mostly forced, even though he self-played a role. Yin suggested Roman Polanski, and Yang rolled his eyes, not a fan of the director. Though they both agreed that he did engage in self-exile, an exile that was based on running from the law, a survival that kept him away from authoritics who wanted to try him for his abuses with young women.

"They moved on to Pablo Neruda, and again, the line between self-imposed and government-imposed exile was blurred. Yes,

Neruda was able to exile himself out of Chile, but it was because the government was seeking his arrest. Yin and Yang found themselves mostly in agreement about government-imposed exiles, Napoleon to both Elba and St. Helena, Seneca and Casanova and Juan Peron. They were so engaged in the movements across borders and political backgrounds of these folks exiled by both force and choice that they forgot to order lunch, finished two beers each, until the appearance of a waiter reminded them they were hungry, and they ordered Moo shu pork with extra pancakes and Gan bian green beans and hot-and-sour soup.

"When the green tea ice cream arrived with fortune cookies Yang thought they had exhausted exile for the day, might move on to a new topic, one fueled by full stomachs with minds fogged by alcohol. But Yin smiled, said, 'What about J. D. Salinger?' and they were at it again for another half hour as the owner turned the *Open* sign to *Closed*, locked the door, allowed them the time they needed to reach closure, these two customers who were regulars, loyal, who spent money, and who livened the place up, others often listening in to what they had to say. Which was sometimes difficult for Yin, whose shyness had never really left him behind, but natural for Yang who, as you already know, loved the dialectic, loves the dialectic. But the second beer Yang always ordered for them helped loosen Yin, open himself up, care less about the surrounding tables and more about the topic at hand with Yang.

"'What about Salinger?' Yang finally answered. 'Do we not think he qualifies?' Yin continued. 'Say more,' Yang said. 'Well, he disappeared from public life for, how many years, thirty or forty. Wouldn't we call that a self-exile? Wouldn't those in the literary world call that a self-exile?' Yang sat back, stretched his arms up and over his chest and shoulders, thought about ordering a third beer. 'Are you suggesting that a man who lives on acreage in New Hampshire, who walks up a hill on his property to a cabin not far from his own house is truly in exile?' Yin smiled, rolled his head on his neck, moved in closer, his forehead now near Yang's. 'Yes, I am. Anything that one does or has done to him or her, that removes them from daily engagement with others, whether friend or foe, qualifies as exile for me. If I stood up, walked across the room, sat at another table far away from you, let's say to avoid digging deeper into this conversation, wouldn't you consider that an exile of sorts?' Yang nodded his head twice, not the type of nod that suggests affirmation, but the type that says I'm thinking about this. 'I'm not sure yet what I think, but I'm willing to consider it.'

"They went on for another hour about Salinger and choices and what it is that people might hide from, why they might exile themselves to a private place where they don't have to deal with what they've done or what others think of them. Yin finally said, 'Have we wrung this one out yet?' Yang loaded his backpack, put on his hat and said, 'I don't think so. Do you know the software program Inspiration?' He didn't. 'What's our topic for next month?' Yang asked.

"As they walked out the door, the proprietor turning the *Closed* sign around to *Open* for the dinner crowd, Yin said, 'How about curiosity?' 'Yes, please,' Yang said."

28

INTERVIEW WITH BOOKSMITH

"WE WILL NOT GIVE YOU OUR REAL NAMES. That's private information. We've always been very private people."

"That's right. Nailed right to the front of our door is one of those 'No Solicitors' signs our nephew bought for us."

"So, you'll get no real names from us. You can call us BookSmith, because that's what we do."

"We make books. As you can tell by our looks, we are twin sisters, born on November 29, 1927. I'm ninety-three years old. So is she."

"What were the names of the two birds on the Red Skelton show that he always joked about? Damn! I can't remember. Little things like that slip away."

"But I remember. That's why we're good for each other. One might forget, but the other might remember. Gertrude, and Heathcliff. Pelicans, I think."

"That's right. Gertrude and Heathcliff. Seagulls. They were seagulls. I'll be Gertrude. You be Heathcliff. Together we'll be BookSmiths. Because we are. We have always worked in the smithing of books."

"You know, he made the transition, too. Later in life."

"Who did what? Don't speak to me in riddles."

"She says that all the time now. The speaking-in-riddles thing. Just because she doesn't understand something or can't follow what I've said, she has to make like I've done something wrong, like I've left something out. Red Skelton! He started painting his art right near the end of World War II."

"Oh, that's right. I had forgotten about that. They estimated he had over one thousand paintings when he died. What kind of Smith would you have called him? ArtSmith?"

"How about ClownSmith? I think that might have been more fitting."

"I do think you're correct, Gertrude! I loved his clown bits."

"Why thank you, Heathcliff. But I don't think she wanted us to talk about Red Skelton, did she?"

"I'm not sure if there are any restrictions. Because we're ninety-three years old, I think we could talk about anything and it would be of interest to her audience. We could talk about the Smothers Brothers. Or Jackie Gleason."

"Or maybe even Dean Martin or Carol Burnett. All of those wonderful variety shows. We'd make a big batch of popcorn, sit down in front of the TV, and settle in for a night of comedy and song."

"When she says big batch of popcorn, she means really big. Big enough to fill a small clothes basket. And we used real butter. Lots of it. Maybe a half a cup. Before they told us how bad butter was for our cholesterol and how it would clog up our veins."

"But look at us. Ninety-three years old, and we'll probably live for another ten or fifteen years. More popcorn, please."

"More butter, please."

"You can see, we have fun. That's always been our motto. 'Have fun!' Whenever one of us went out by ourselves, the other would always say, 'Have fun!'"

"Which wasn't too often. Having been together for nearly ten decades, we like to be together, go out together. It's kind of like agoraphobia, but a little different flavor."

"Right. Like a separation anxiety."

"We tried to date boys back in high school. Had lots of fun. Played games with them. Switched up on them so they never knew if they were with … Gertrude or Heathcliff."

"But we didn't like being alone with them. Never liked where they wanted to take things. Even when we went to college. We roomed together. Stayed to ourselves."

"That's right. Best thing we ever did in our lives. We knew early on we loved making books and wanted to spend the rest of our lives making them."

"We started early. Dad was an art professor, so we always had tons of materials around the house, and he'd often take us to school and let us hang out and create things. I think we were nine when we made our first books. I made one for … Gertrude, using the poetry of Emily Dickinson."

"I still have it. Right next to my side of the bed on the nightstand. And the one I made for Heathcliff came from a book on William Blake. I cut out images and words, even though I didn't understand them very well, and presented it to Heathcliff on our tenth birthday."

"We made books for all our friends, family members, teachers, anybody who showed an interest."

"When Dad took us to work with him, we'd often end up in the university library, studying about book art and artists and places where people went to school to study book art."

"Gertrude here was the first to discover Wells College. Nestled in the middle of New York in a town called Aurora —"

"Situated on Cayuga Lake."

"That's right. By the time we were thirteen years old, we knew we wanted to spend our college years there. We had discovered Victor Hammer. He fled the Nazi regime in Austria in 1939 and found his way to Wells."

"By the way, Wells is named after the guy who created American Express and Wells Fargo Bank."

"We were so lucky to study with Victor, who was a master printer, typographer, calligrapher."

"Yeah, the only problem we had with him was his devotion to God. We've never embodied that devotion, so just kept our mouths shut when he pontificated, knowing that we were there to learn everything he knew about book arts and related areas."

"The year we graduated was the same year he retired. That was 1947. We were in our early twenties."

"Sadly, when he left, the Wells program went quiet."

"Silent! For forty-five years. Not until 1993 did they breathe a little life and money into a new Book Arts Center."

"They contacted us to contribute, which we were happy to do."

"And we send them a new piece of book art every year to help grow their collection."

"They like us."

"That's right. There is no one else left alive on the planet who studied with Victor. They invite us to attend events every year."

"Unfortunately, we don't travel too well anymore. So we'll send an annual donation. Write a nice letter."

"That's where we met our first Vandercook 4 press. Victor loved it. He was always hunting for more, but they were hard to come by."

"When we moved back to California after graduation, we immediately started looking for one. Of course we couldn't afford one yet."

"But we continued to make books, books that received attention quickly when they read our resumes and saw that we were Wells alums."

"And when Gertrude says 'they,' she means the directors of special-collections libraries at universities. They loved our work from day one."

"They put us on their list. Told us to send them a copy of every new edition we put out."

"So we started thinking in terms of editions. We had a couple dozen universities after our work about the time we were thirty years old. We made a down payment on a house."

"Pretty little house with a nice old workshop in the back. That's when I found our Vandercook. I think we paid seven hundred and fifty dollars for it. You know if you go look for one today, they're fifteen thousand. Crazy. The only people who use them anymore are artists, colleges, teachers."

"We've come a long way since then. More than just broadsides and books. We don't drive anymore, but we have friends who take us up to UCSC to Cowell Press, or Mills College where they have a great book art program, led by Julie Chen."

"So much to learn. So many ways to stretch our craft and knowledge. We use magnets for our enclosure work. We go up to the San Francisco Center for the Book and take classes on photopolymer so we don't have to set type anymore."

"These old arthritic fingers don't like setting type. And we bought a laser cutter a couple of years ago. Best thing since buttered popcorn."

"So much fun to play with. You'll find some evidence of the cutting in most of our projects these days."

"We have an edition that should be ready by Christmas, focusing on the life and work of Ruth Bader Ginsburg. We've already sold out the edition of fifty to the special-collections libraries."

"We're a bit slower than we used to be, but the quality gets better all the time. We have interns from the university who come down and run the press for us. Not enough muscles in these arms anymore to crank the cylinder."

"They learn a lot from us. We learn a lot from them."

"When we finish the RBG project, we're moving on to a Black Lives Matter series that the local museum is already planning to display for Black History Month in February."

"We keep busy. These important projects that need to make their way into the world keep us waking up every morning, grabbing our two cups of heavily caffeinated coffee, and making our way out into the workshop."

"We know we have a limited timeline. Not too many people on the planet make it to one hundred years old. But we've been good to ourselves. Good to our bodies."

"Except for the damn butter on the popcorn, we've been smart, sensible. Never eat red meat. Mostly veggies from our garden. Fish we have students bring us from the harbor."

"So we're thinking in terms of seven years. Two or three projects a year. Just need to prioritize what we think are the most important topics to share with the world."

"Yeah. I guess we need to deal with this COVID thing. It's part of our lives."

"Not so much part of our lives, except for the three of us sitting here with masks on. We don't get out much anyway. But it's certainly a part of everyone else's lives, so eventually, we'll need to address it."

"But I want to go back to William Blake. Showcase him in an edition. He really started so much of it. And Kenneth Patchen. Love his stuff."

"And Maya Angelou."

"And Ocean Vuong."

"I don't know Ocean Vuong."

"You will. I downloaded his book *On Earth We're Briefly Gorgeous* this morning. I thought we could start it during lunch today."

"What is for lunch today?"

"Brie-and-avocado panini. Corn chowder. Cherie and Pam from Cowell Press are coming down today to work on the Ruth project and they're cooking for us."

"Oh, how lovely! What a life we've had. Continue to have."
"You've got that right, my sweet sister."

29

INTERVIEW WITH
BLACKSMITH

"WHILE I HAVE NEVER HELD a cross-pein hammer in my hands, or slammed any type of hammer into an anvil, I think it's best for the purposes of your study that you call me BlackSmith, as I would be willing to bet that I'm the first black person you've interviewed and the name is still available. And if we want to be metaphorical, we might want to think about the possible synonyms for blacksmith — like smithy, farrier, plover, shoer, and my favorite, forger. Not that any of these help you with the goals of your project, though in reading your introductory paragraph, I'm not certain I understand what your goals are.

"What I do understand is that you would like me to tell you about myself, my life, in terms of the everyman usc of the name Smith. In other words, what are the personal aspects of my life that lend themselves to the universals that you are attempting to capture. I don't know if I can be that direct, that linear, to squeeze myself into your frame. Instead I may just ramble a bit, let you listen, as is your wont, let you figure out whether or not my thoughts qualify as a good fit with your needs.

"If we had convened this interview, or I should say this monologue, a few months earlier, the content and flow would be much different than what you'll hear me say today. I'm sure you understand what I mean. For example, how uncomfortable do you think I feel, as a black man, a fairly large black man weighing in excess of two hundred twenty-five pounds, walking into my bank, a bank I've frequented for twenty-five years, wearing a mask. I almost feel like I need to raise my hands over my shoulders, lay them flat against the top of my head, keep them exposed so nobody thinks I might have a concealed weapon that I might pull out at any time to accomplish my desire to rob the bank. I have never owned a gun, never touched a gun in my life, not even a BB gun as a child. As far back as I can remember, I don't think I've ever worn a mask. I never dressed up at Halloween as Darth Vader or Zorro or the Phantom of the Opera. But today, I am living a new reality, in an existence that requires the wearing of masks, in a world that increasingly struggles with the notion of Black Lives Matter.

"The one devastates me. The existence on the planet of COVID-19 that demands a level of safety to attempt to control a brutal disease that is killing millions of folks across the planet. It is out of control. There is nothing I can do about it but wait. Wait to see if a vaccine is created. Wait to see if I will receive a dose when it's ready. Wait to see if I will test positive, or if any member of my family, or friends, will get sick and require isolated treatment, or die.

"The other one also devastates me. That the degree of racism and bigotry in our country, in our world, would breed the need for a slogan that reads Black Lives Matter. On July 13, 2013, a handful of activists created this slogan with the hope of disrupting business as usual. They did so. And with it came a flood of controversy. Those that said in response 'All Lives

Matter.' To be honest with you, the slogan bothered me in the beginning. I thought of my Hispanic friends, wondered if they were thinking, Don't Brown Lives Matter as well? What about Yellow Lives and Red Lives? And until the murder of George Floyd by a sanctioned police officer, the Black Lives Matter controversy still existed. But now, with the whole world as witness to the final breath Floyd squeaked out under the knee of Derek Chauvin, there is a much deeper and widespread understanding to the meaning of Black Lives Matter. An understanding by white folks who have existed in the wake of institutional racism that nothing will change until they make a difference in their own lives, their own politics, their own way of living that helps to end unwarranted bigotry and hatred.

"But here I go. On a soapbox now. Not telling you what I think you want to hear about me as black everyman. What would have been a slightly different story back in March before we were asked to shelter in place, and a radically different story before Floyd's murder on May 25th. But let me try to recall that previous existence for you. I live in a liberally progressive town and work at a university. For the most part, I do not feel the direct implications of racism. I have white friends, Asian friends, Native friends, trans friends. But I'm lucky. I don't live in Minneapolis or Atlanta or other places where hatred of folks because of the color of their skin or the way they speak is rampant. I'm a father. I'm a soccer coach. I play racquetball with a Korean man and a Vietnamese woman. I attend Pie for the People gatherings where I eat pie and donate to a cause that supports issues I believe in. You might think that in this town, this fairyland existence, I might forget that I'm black. Never the case. I grew up in East Oakland before making my way south to this Shangri-la. Every day of my life from preschool through high school I experienced one flavor or another of racism directed at me from classmates simply because my skin looked different than theirs.

"But let's move on from this political emphasis. Let me tell you about my addictions. That could take more time than you have left to use up with me. The reason why I'm climbing up the scale close to two hundred and fifty pounds has everything to do with ice cream. And not just any ice cream. I started with Edy's, switched over to Haagen Dazs. Pretty quickly. But that was before a vacation the family took in 2016 to Jackson Hole, Wyoming. First thing we discovered there — well, after the moose and elk — was Cream and Sugar artisan ice cream. It is literally to die for, and if I'm not careful that may happen sooner than I like. It was one thing to get addicted live and in person in a handful of restaurants that carried their six flavors. But it was a whole other thing to discover that right here from my California home, I could order the six-pack for ninety-nine dollars with a guarantee to have it delivered to my table within three days. Just the six original flavors, but I get all of them: chocolate, cookies and cream, huckleberry, mint chocolate chip, salted caramel, and vanilla. I will sit on the porch waiting for the UPS truck to pull up to my driveway. Hell, once I was so jaded, I used that new Follow My Delivery program they send out to preferred customers, and starting at noon I could see the truck slowly moving my way, make it up to the housing tract a half mile from my house, slowly wind its way up the hill to where I live, until I finally see it just around the corner, less than half a mile from my doorstep. I began to salivate, had to stand up and walk around the yard picking weeds to keep busy. Forty-five minutes later, while looking at the map, the truck just around the corner hadn't moved. I was not happy. How was that possible? I went into the house, picked up the Warriors mask my wife had made me, and walked around the corner. I saw the UPS truck sitting there, the driver nowhere to be seen. I kept thinking about my ice cream inside waiting for me. After fifteen more minutes I was so riled up I walked up to the door of the house where the truck was parked and knocked. A man a little older than me came to the door. I could see over his shoulder that the driver was sitting at the kitchen table, shoes off, eating from a plate of food. Before I could say anything, the driver's mother stuck her face out the door and said, 'My son works a long day, and he deserves the right to his dinner time uninterrupted.' I said something stupid then left. It took another forty-five minutes before my ice cream showed up. I ate the salted caramel top to bottom, wouldn't share a bite with anyone.

"But that's not my serious addiction. It's the one my wife tries to curb, worries about raising my blood sugar. My primary addiction has no sharp edges, won't affect my body negatively, should affect everyone positively. If they understood as I do. I would teach everyone if they allowed me in. The only possible disadvantages to this addiction could be economic, if you indulge to the degree that I do, or the time sink that can occur when one's wife tells him that he is overdoing it.

"In my humble opinion, there is no way to overdo an appreciation for blues harmonica. I first heard Paul Butterfield play. My first taste was at Fillmore West in San Francisco. Six of us drove across the Bay Bridge and, just as we found a parking spot, somebody brought out a joint, and we smoked it to the nub before we walked in. Elvin Bishop was just finishing their set, and up walked Paul Butterfield onto the stage. When he touched that harmonica to his lips and started to blow, I almost melted into the floor. Maybe it was the pot, but I didn't care. I was an instant convert, a disciple for life, of not only Butterfield, who died much too young in 1987, but of every blues harmonica player that had ever lived or was still alive. I made it my mission to hear every player ever recorded, and to see as many as I could, even if it meant taking out a loan and jumping on a plane. Junior Wells, James Cotton, Big Walter Horton. I missed out on Sonny Boy Williamson and Little Walter, both dying a few years before I discovered my drug of choice. Even when I moved here, there was a club called O. T. Price and somehow they landed big-time acts. I saw Charlie Musselwhite and Norton Buffalo there on the same night. I even made it up to the city in the early eighties to hear Sonny Terry. He may be the best of all of them. As you can imagine, I have a very large cabinet in my living room containing

45s, LPs, tapes, and videos of every harmonica player I've ever heard of. This is an addiction I enjoy living with. And a good thing about it, it doesn't matter what color your skin is. Any color, any gender, can jump aboard and fill your veins with the blues."

30

Interview between WordSmith and LadySmith

"Thanks so much for sharing your first twenty-nine interviews with me. This is quite an accomplishment, especially given the gap that occurred between mid-March and now, when the world veered off its course in more ways than one. Did you ever imagine when you started this journey that you'd end up with content like you got from BlackSmith? Or that we'd be wearing masks for our talk today?"

"To be honest, what I never imagined is that I would be allowing myself to talk like this with you at all."

"I understand. It was clear that as time went on you were trying to remove yourself from the narrative. Until now. Until allowing a co-conspirator like me into the fray."

"Right. Though I still have editorial control over what I include in my final report to the foundation."

"Ah! I see. So you will red-pencil out what you don't like of this discourse we are engaging in. Or, you might just slice the whole interview and pretend like it never happened."

"I have a feeling that, regardless of what I keep in the report, I won't be able to pretend that what you and I will engage in now never happened, Yin says to Yang."

"Very good! And are you wanting to play Yin or Yang?"

"As I understand it after listening to your interview a half-dozen times, I don't think it matters which role I play. What does matter to me, though, is that we continue to unravel the mystery of Smith as the previous interviews have done."

"Indeed! I will stick with my WordSmith moniker, while occasionally assuming the role of Yang when it seems fitting."

"And I will continue to use LadySmith, and would be happy to function as the Yin to your Yang as the scene demands."

"When you interviewed me back in early March — wait, let me clarify. When I spewed to you in unfamiliar fashion a monologue without a companion with whom to enter into the dialectic, I created a Yin with whom I could interact. One of the topics I mentioned was an immersion into word studies."

"Correct. And I believe the last word study you engaged in with your friend Yin focused on the word, the concept, of 'exile.'

"That's right. But we finished that idea, ended with a disagreement on whether or not J.D. Salinger's behavior was an agreed-on representation of exile. Are you ready, my dear friend Yin, to embark on the study of a new word, a concept that wholly fascinates me, partly because I had never heard the word before reading the introductory page of your intended study, and partly because as I began to focus on it, it felt slippery, like a slimy fish that avoids your grasp, a concept that could outgrow my Inspiration mind map and spread like this current virus of ours, to every region of the mind, to every city in the world?"

"I'm ready."

"Are you sure?"

"What have I got to lose?"

"Indeed! Then on we go, into the expansive and murky world of … fictography."

"Oh, no! You can't do that. That's my world. My heart and soul. The thread I grasp for when my head leaves the world I think I'm inhabiting and find myself in a sinkhole with no means of escape."

"I assure you we will find an exit that keeps us both alive, and seeking more."

"I don't like it, but as promised, I am here for you. Fire away."

"I will choose a different metaphor, as there are already way too many idioms and adages that focus on the use of guns and other weapons of mass, or even minor, destruction, so instead of firing away, I will commence on a journey that requires both Yin and Yang to construct a world scaffolded with other concepts and words that help to prop up and support our word of choice, which I restate, for both of our ears to rejoice in, so the pathways and tunnels and orifices through which we might come to know fictography will provide us smooth entry, allow us to bounce off walls without encumbering bruises, without slipping on shiny pebbles in our way, without finding our tongue tied in purple knots that inhibit speech and suggest blockage, instead striding forth with confidence into an unknown realm, one where kings and queens and servants and chefs stand toe to toe and find their way forward."

"That was quite a mouthful. Is this how it will go?"

"It will go however and wherever Yin and Yang choose to respond, or not, to each other. For now, I believe it is up to you to place the first stone on this imaginary Go board of ours, given that the word belongs to you, originated with you, one I have never heard until being asked to participate in this fascinating enigmatic study of yours — fictography, my friend, Yin, in your hands."

"I don't know that it is in my hands. I agree that I had never heard the word before it released itself from my fingertips into a willing keyboard as I wrote the first draft of my white paper to submit to foundations about this idea that grew out of a restless night's sleep that kept putting ideas into my head until I finally forced my feet to the floor and found my computer, the cursor throbbing, expecting me, waiting for me to jump in and make some sense out of a senseless world."

"That's the Yin I know. A cautious but intentional placement of white stones to commence the game. Let me take my turn. I move into the dictionary to discover the etymological roots of *ficto*, which I find comes from the Latin *fictus*, which on first blush means 'to form.' Digging deeper I find a bit of a darker meaning, hiding in shadows: 'a deliberate lie or untruth.'"

"I find that darkness puzzling, if not entirely inaccurate, in the description of my own fictography. But given your attempt to encircle sections of our board with your own logically placed black stones, it seems I must continue down a similar path and unbury the beginnings of *graphy*, which in English means a field of study related directly to writing."

"Yes, indeed, my friend. "To form a deliberate lie or untruth through writing."

"Or talking, as we are doing now. To use the word 'deliberate' is an assumption I'm not willing to make, or even the use of the word 'lie' as a descriptor in the creation of the word. My fictography has more organic origins."

"Now you introduce another pathway of research, given that 'organic' comes from the Greek, meaning relating to an organ or instrument. Do we want to let ourselves slide down that slope, dear Yin, or might we modify your stated origins?"

"I do not believe that 'we' would be able to make such modifications. I believe if such modifications were useful to the future of our discussion, it would be 'me' who makes them."

"You play this game well, as I suspected, as I gleaned from reading your initial explanation to the foundation about your need for funding for this unique, and shall I say, important work."

"We slip deeper into a series of segues that threatens to move us further from our intended goals. But for now, I will enjoy the slippage, like a slide at a water park whose intentions are to shake me up, splash me into something new and unexpected. I'll proceed on your 'important work' statement and agree that at first, I believed that the work to be completed was in fact important, even vital, at least to me, to my then-current existence as well as future implications for what my work might become."

"Are you saying that you are no longer clear about the importance of your work having now conducted and completed it?"

"That's not fair. You'll influence the outcome of my study."

"Hasn't every interview you've conducted influenced the outcome of your study?"

"Yes, but not with intent."

"Oh, what a good word. Can we save 'intent' for a future discussion?"

"When you first asked, actually demanded, I agreed to one discussion with you."

"I'm certain by the time we're done, you'll be the one demanding more."

"We'll see, but back to your question. Not exactly. At different points in the capturing of details and facts throughout the series of interviews, I questioned the veracity of my premise, but never lost a view toward its value, its importance. To climb back up the rabbit hole, let me make my way back to organic origins. Because I don't want to argue for a connection to an organ or instrument, I will modify my earlier supposition and say that my definition of fictography had its origins emanating from tea bags, from shots of whiskey late at night as the ink dried up, as I read and wrote and struggled with the accuracy of biographies and autobiographies and literary works of fiction."

"The closest thing Yang has seen to your coinage of the term 'fictography' is 'autofiction.' When we follow the thread, we discover that it found its way into life and our vocabulary in a blurb on the back of the French novelist Serge Doubrovsky's book *Fils*. It appears that the new word had to do with a blending of the real and invented. I think your word is better, has more layers, more room for nuance and experimentation. As you described it in interview number nineteen with yourself, fictography functions as a blade with many different surfaces, the ability to cut deeply and gush blood or just brush the surface and remove hairs from skin. It fascinates me and I'm so happy to be having this discussion with you."

"It also thrills me, and that Yin and Yang can toss this about like a well-tuned Frisbee makes me quite excited. Nearly two hundred pages now define this work, and I sometimes think about crumpling them up and using them to ignite kindling. When I reread the pages, I wonder about the speakers' truths, about what they know, what they don't know, what they fabricate, what they invent, or what they steal. But for me, under the guise of fictography, all of that is perfectly acceptable."

"What percentage of your work, not just this study, but of everything you've ever written or recorded, would you call fictography?"

"Easy answer. One hundred percent. Same with yours. I have read so much of your work, as a writer, as a teacher of writing, as an activist and a thinker, and as articulate as you are, I would still say that every word you have ever written qualifies as fictography. Really, every word ever written on this planet qualifies as fictography."

"Such a fascinating concept! Yet one so difficult to prove. What evidence have you gleaned from these interviews that supports your premise?"

"I don't know that I've proved anything with the results of this work. Mostly satisfied my curiosity. I've never felt the need for proof about my fictography theory, because I'm firmly entrenched in my belief. What I have been more interested in is the nature of everyman, that the range of behavior and beliefs and actions of the Smiths in my life are so dissimilar in so many ways, and yet so similar in other ways. Probably what I've learned more than anything is that thirty interviews is far too few. I may need to append the title with Volume One."

"My dear, Yin, I find your ideas and discourse fascinating, a worthy collaborator in the seeking of truths. I look forward to more."

"As do I, Yang. I believe you have already identified our next area of study: 'intent.'"

CONCLUSION

T O SATISFY THE CONDITIONS OF MY STUDY and receive appropriate remuneration, I was required to submit an online assessment that detailed the accomplishments and difficulties with the implementation of the original design. It was clear, given the structure of their template, that they were interested in determining if "Eclectic" was a viable category for future funding. It was also clear that the foundation was looking at potential future funding for projects that continued to engender curiosity. A series of details were required first, as evidenced in the chart below:

Categories	Details	Notes
Project Title	*Smith: An Unauthorized Fictography*	Might add Volume 1
# of Interviews	30	
# of Males	15	#30 - two subjects
# of Females	17	#28 - twins as subjects
# of Words	62,366	Including conclusion
# of Pages	208	Double-spaced
Author Voice involved	20	#1-19 and # 30
"Smith" uses	303	
"Fictography" uses	28	Including plurals

Categories	Details	Notes
"Unauthorized" uses	11	
Accomplishments (up to 3)		
1. Eliminating myself from the narrative in interviews 20 through 29.		
2. Completing 30 interviews even though COVID-19 got in the way.		
3. Successful survey of 30 Smiths and how they each embodied the notion of everyman.		
Difficulties (up to 3)		
1. Interview 7 with TechSmith was terminated early. He was belligerent and resistant to participate.		
2. The untimely appearance of COVID-19 after interview 27.		
3. Being a narrative element in the first 19 interviews and interview 30.		
Surprises (up to 3)		
1. That I allowed myself to participate in interview 30 with WordSmith, not really an interview, but more of a dialectic.		
2. How much I enjoyed interview 30 with WordSmith.		
3. How interview 30 changed my mindset about future possibilities: intent.		
The Future		
Based upon my analysis of the 30 Smiths who participated in the study, I believe that the concepts of "Smith," "unauthorized," and "fictography" deserve additional focus. I'm proposing an additional two years' worth of studies represented by 60 interviews to appear in Volumes 2 and 3. An additional area of focus discovered through my final discussion with WordSmith in interview 30 is the notion of "intent." In this first study, I was clear about my intent, but ignored the intent of the interviewees. In the future studies, understanding and pursuit of the intentions of the interviewees will be a key component. I look forward to the possibility of continuing to work with you.		

I haven't heard back from the foundation regarding future funding, but I have been meeting regularly with WordSmith wearing homemade masks at a social distance of twelve feet on the patio of the Crow's Nest restaurant.

About the Author

Jory Post was an educator, writer, and artist who lived in Santa Cruz, California. He and his wife, Karen Wallace, created handmade books and art together as JoKa Press. Jory was the co-founder and publisher of *phren-z*, an online literary quarterly, and founder of the *Zoom Forward* reading series.

His first book of prose poetry, *The Extra Year*, was published in 2019, and was followed by a second, *Of Two Minds*, in 2020. His novel, *Pious Rebel*, also appeared in 2020.

His work has been published in *Catamaran Literary Reader, Chicago Quarterly Review, Rumble Fish Quarterly, The Sun*, and elsewhere. His short stories "Sweet Jesus" and "Hunt and Gather" were nominated for the Pushcart Prize.

ALSO BY JORY POST

PIOUS REBEL

After her partner dies suddenly, Lisa Hardrock realizes how little she knows about the life she's been living — and starts exploring her questions in a blog that unexpectedly goes viral.

Available from Paper Angel Press in
hardcover, trade paperback, and digital editions
paperangelpress.com